HOUSE OF FLESH

HOUSE
OF
FLESH

BRUNO FISCHER

BRUIN BOOKS
THE EMERALD EMPIRE
EUGENE, OREGON

Published by
Bruin Books, LLC
March, 2011

This book was designed and edited by Jonathan Eeds
Graphics design by Michelle Policicchio

Special thanks to Nora (Fischer) Kisch & Adam Fischer

Printed in the United States of America
ISBN 978-0-9826339-6-0
Bruin Books, LLC
Eugene, Oregon, USA

Visit the scene of the crime at www.bruinbookstore.com

If the heats of hate and lust

In the house of flesh are strong,

Let me mind the house of dust

Where my sojourn shall be long.

A Shropshire Lad by A. E. Housman.

Chapter One »»»

I LAY ON THE LAWN and watched Conrad Hickey paint a nude. She was an Amazon with a luscious hourglass figure and skin like strawberry juice. She looked as if she could break a man in half, and that wasn't all she looked good for.

"Friend of yours?" I asked.

Mr. Hickey chuckled. "Call her an aging man's daydream."

She looked more my size—in height, anyway. Mr. Hickey was small-framed, with a pinched pixie face and a fey glint in his blue eyes. The way he had painted her, he would just about have reached to her shoulder. I wondered why the runty elderly ones hankered for women big and blowzy and with skin like strawberry juice.

With the palette poised in his left hand, he peered into space as if the model were standing before us in the flesh. Regrettably, she wasn't. He had copied the outlines of her from a fairly sedate photo of somebody or other in a magazine, and his paint brushes had stripped the clothes off her.

I didn't know whether Conrad Hickey was any good as an artist. He told me that he had no opinion on the subject either, but that it was more fun than practicing law, from which he had retired a couple of years ago to devote himself to painting red barns in sunlight and country roads flanked by silver birches, and naked women.

There were plenty of roads and barns, but no professional models, so he used his lively and ribald imagination to paint nudes.

Jessica Hickey appeared on the porch to shake out a dust mop.

She was cut to her husband's size except that she was better padded, without being plump—a gray-haired woman who, already deep in her fifties, could wear shorts and jersey sweaters without distressing the eye. She was amiable and seasoned and the nicest landlady I'd ever had.

"Don't let him kid you, Harry," she called from the porch. She smoked incessantly and seldom removed her cigarette when she spoke. "He never knew a woman like that."

"I don't expect anybody did," I said. "When they're that fleshy, they're sloppy, except in paintings."

"The boy's a philosopher," Mr. Hickey commented. He applied dark-brown paint to a huge breast. "Jessica, someday I'm going to paint you."

"If you try, I'll break your damn neck," Mrs. Hickey said placidly and flicked ashes from her cigarette and returned into the gray clapboard house.

I turned over on my stomach. It was a scorching day in early July. The only cool spot was here with Mr. Hickey under a huge sugar maple. I felt rested and at peace after ten days in North Set.

Dave Morrison, the Gothams' coach, had picked this place for me. Jessica Hickey was his aunt.

"They've a one-room bungalow near their house," Dave

had told me. "I used to stay there. Kitchen, bath, electricity, plumbing, fireplace. They haven't rented it out lately because they don't want close neighbors, but Aunt Jessica will let you have it if I ask her. It's the place for you to spend the summer. Far enough from New York so you won't keep running in, and no tourists for you to raise hell with. Take a box of books and a batch of those double-crostic crossword puzzles that I never knew anybody but you could do, and lie in the sun and put on weight. The village is so small there'll be few if any women available, but, if you do happen to latch onto one, for heaven's sake don't take her seriously."

So far it had worked out fine. When it rained, I did double-crostics or read. When it was bright and hot like today, I lay about outside or went swimming at Twin Rock. And there was a girl who so far had helped spend two evenings. Her name was Polly Wellman and she was the post-master's daughter. Once I had taken her to the movies in Fort Able and once I had taken her dancing, and each time I had kissed her good night. No more than that, and I didn't intend it to be.

"You have company," Mr. Hickey announced. Then he whistled like a schoolboy. "Golly, would I like to paint that!"

I turned on my side. My bungalow was a couple of hundred feet from the Hickey house and back a piece from the road. Parked behind my coupe on the battered, rutted dirt driveway was a snappy convertible with the top down. Gale was getting out of it.

"Yoo-hoo, darling," she called.

Mr. Hickey smirked. "Is she yours, Harry?"

"Not any more." I stood up and brushed leaves and twigs from my chest. I wasn't wearing anything but shorts and sneakers.

"What a pity," he said. "She doesn't look like someone a young man would enjoy being without."

"That's what you think," I growled and started toward her.

I knew the car wasn't hers. She must have borrowed it from some man. There were always men anxious to lend her anything they had.

Gale was posing for me. She leaned lightly against the door of the convertible and had the proper smile on her orange mouth. She wore a cool white linen blouse with rhinestone buttons and a black pleated skirt.

No hat went with the black veil that was over her face and caught under her chin and tied up over her blonde hair to restrain it while driving in an open car. She was an advertising model, and glamorous effects were her stock in trade.

When I reached her, she moved from the car and rose to her toes to kiss me lightly through the veil. At that, I had to dip my head to meet her mouth, but I kept my hands away from her.

She stepped back and looked me over. "I can see your ribs," she said critically.

I said, "What the hell do you want?"

Gale pouted. I could have anticipated that pout.

"Why, Hair-y, is that the way to speak to a woman who was your wife until so recently?"

At the beginning, I had found it cute the way she pronounced my name Hair-y. I didn't any more.

"How did you manage to track me down and why?" I demanded.

"I phoned your sister Rose in Queens, and she told me where you were staying. Darling, you're a fast worker. She's crazy over you."

"You can't mean my sister."

"The girl in the post office here in North Set. I stopped there to ask for directions. When I told her I was looking for you, she suddenly didn't like me. Jealousy, if ever I saw it. But darling, isn't she a little too starry-eyed and young for you?"

I didn't get a chance to tell her to mind her own business. Something warm and moist touched my bare ankle. I looked down and saw a little black dog nuzzling me.

"Beat it," I said, waving my foot.

"Hair-y, don't kick Max!"

"Who?" I said.

"Max. My dog. He's the reason I drove all the way up here from New York."

"Since when have you had a dog?"

"Since six weeks ago. May Burgess gave him to me. Isn't he adorable?"

The dog's tongue lolled. His black coat was too thick for that kind of weather. He had a white blaze over a muzzle that was ridiculously long and a stubby tail that wagged passionately when he noticed me looking down at him. I didn't think he was adorable.

"Of course Max is just a mutt," Gale explained as if that needed explanation, "but I love him. The trouble is they won't let him in my apartment. The neighbors complain that he barks at night, and the superintendent says that either Max or both of us will have to leave, and you know how scarce apartments are in New York."

"So I'm it, huh?"

"Do you mind, darling? After all, he'll keep you company."

"I don't want company."

"The poor thing has nowhere else to go and he'll love it in the country. I borrowed this car from Hank Pierce and drove three hours in this heat just to bring him to you." She put an orange-tipped hand on my chest. "Darling, you can't be so mean."

"What happens to him after the summer?"

"I'll work something out."

I was stuck. "All right," I said.

And that was the beginning. For me, anyway, though it had started before that. But the chances are that I wouldn't have got into it if it hadn't been for the dog.

Gale wasn't through with me. She didn't go right back to the city and leave me in peace. She took off her veil and opened two rhinestone buttons of her blouse and said: "I'm roasting. Isn't there a place where I can take a swim before I start back?"

"In what?"

"I happened to bring my bathing suit." She dipped into the convertible and came out with a tiny weekend bag and sailed into my bungalow with the dog at her heels.

I had no choice. Gale looked around the bungalow and said it was charming and opened the rest of her blouse. What she wore under it was transparent. I fetched my trunks and went into the bathroom.

It took me only a few seconds. Then I leaned against the basin and waited for her to change in the other room. I wished she hadn't come. She messed me up. It wasn't that I loved her. Maybe I never had—not even at the beginning.

Last fall, I had met her for the first time in a restaurant near Madison Square Garden after a game. She was at a table with some people I knew, and one of the men called me over and said she wanted to meet me. She had watched me play that evening. It turned out that she was a basketball fan and she kept telling how she had admired my speed and my ball handling. As a matter of fact, I'd had a poor evening, but I liked to hear praise from her, and, even more than that, I liked to look at her. I took her home and went up to her apartment for a nightcap. A couple of weeks later, we were married.

At first, it had been pretty good. We had one thing in common: we enjoyed making love to each other. But there was nothing else. The experts on sex tell you that's what you need for a successful marriage, but that's not all you need. If it could have been arranged for us to be married two hours out of every twenty-four—say between one and three a.m.— it would have worked out. The rest of the time, we became increasingly bored with each other and carpingly picked on each other and had shouting battles, and that affected the sex part. In March, we agreed on a divorce.

"Hair-y, are you going to stay in there all day?" Gale called.

I came out. She was wearing a knee-length beach robe and slippers. She had wonderful long, slender legs. Max chased those legs to the door.

"You'd better lock him in till he becomes familiar with the place," she said.

"Does he know enough to go to the bathroom?"

"Max is a very intelligent dog."

I closed the door in his disappointed face. Under the maple tree, Conrad Hickey was working with a sketch pad. He leered at me. There was a short cut to Twin Rock by footpath through the woods, but I took her the long way by road so that we could drive.

The pool was a natural formation in a hollow formed by

ledge rock bisected by the creek, which was dammed up at the upstream end. The water was transparent and crisply cool and deep enough for diving. On either side there was a broad expanse of flat ledge, where the swimmers could sun themselves.

Because of the blazing heat, the crowd was larger than usual. In ten days, I had become slightly acquainted with a few of the villagers, but those I nodded to weren't the only ones who stared at Gale as we came up on the nearer ledge. She inevitably drew gazes, from men as well as women. But that was nothing to what happened when she dropped her robe.

Gale's bathing suit only approximated one. It consisted of a skimpy white cloth wound about her loins and a narrower strip partially across her magnificent breasts. It was the kind of thing worn by the more daring on the beaches of the French Riviera, but it was hardly the sort of attire for a creek in a small and highly conventional village. North Set wasn't a tourist place where natives got used to that sort of thing. So they stared—the older women scandalized, the younger women envious, the men of all ages enraptured. It was the exact effect Gail wanted.

I could have spanked her. I was going to live here for a couple of more months. I turned from her and dove.

She followed me. She turned on her back and floated, and because what she wore was almost the color of her skin she looked, in the darker water, as if she was wearing nothing. I swam away from her. After a few minutes, I climbed out by myself.

She wasn't lonely in the pool. She was treading water and talking with a man. His hair was even lighter than hers, sticking up short and thick in a crew haircut. He was handsome, of course. Gale didn't waste time on men who weren't. I had never seen him before. I didn't give a damn.

A few minutes later, they were out of the water on the opposite ledge. She lay on her back and he sat at her side. The rest of him was now visible. He was as tall as I, but his ribs didn't show. He was all chest and biceps. She laughed a great deal, but his square-jawed, classic face never cracked. He looked sort of stupid. In that case, he and Gale should get along fine.

I turned over and let the sun bake my back.

"She might as well be stark naked," a woman's prim voice said. "And imagine Dr. Doane carrying on with her in public."

A doctor, no less. I doubted that that would be an improvement over a professional basketball player. I looked sideways along my forearm. Two middle-aged women sat near me. As they spoke, they kept staring at Gale and Nature Boy on the opposite ledge.

"Have you heard what they say happened to his first wife?" the second one said.

Her companion nodded with grim excitement. "They say he fed her to his—"

Then she noticed me listening and broke off. Their voices dropped to whispers.

I lay in the sun and wondered vaguely what had been fed to what. I wasn't much interested. I must have dozed off because the next thing I knew Gale's hand was on my shoulder.

"Hair-y, let's take one more dip and go. I've a long drive."

Bending over me like that, she practically spilled out of herself. I sat up. Evidently her boyfriend had gone.

I dove into the water with her. I was used to an audience when I was on a basketball court, not when I swam. But of course, I wasn't the one they were looking at.

As we drove back to the bungalow, I said sourly: "Wasn't that bathing suit enough to induce Nature Boy to stick a-round?"

She handed me a coy glance. "Why, darling, I declare you're jealous."

"Like hell I am."

"He's cute," she said contentedly.

"So I've been hearing. Seems he has a cute habit of—"

I didn't know how to finish it. That snatch of conversation I had heard on the ledge didn't make sense. One of the women had started to say that he had fed his wife to his something, and then had stopped there. I must have heard it wrong. You didn't feed a wife to something; you fed her something, especially when you were a doctor and could more easily get away with it. A fascinating theory.

"What were you saying about him, Hair-y?"

"Nothing." I didn't know enough about it—in fact, anything about it—for even a feeble wisecrack.

Max went crazy when we came into the bungalow. He must have thought himself abandoned in a strange place. He jumped at Gale as if trying to knock her down, and he had a wag of his tail left over for me. She threw off her robe and hugged him and kissed him somewhat more ardently than she used to hug and kiss me. My stomach turned over a little. I went to the table for a cigarette.

"It's almost six o'clock," she said when she rose. "How about taking me out to dinner before I start back?"

"There's no decent restaurant in miles. You get dressed while I make coffee and throw together some sandwiches."

I put the coffee on then set the table in the living room. She remained in her damp bathing suit, standing at the built-in bookshelf and studying the titles of my books—just as if she had read anything but advertisements since the sixth grade. I went back into the kitchen to make ham and cheese sandwiches on rye.

When I brought out the sandwiches, the two white pieces of her bathing suit were on the floor. She hadn't bothered to go into the bathroom to change and she hadn't yet put anything on. Her back was to me, and, familiar as that picture was, it hadn't lost any of its charm.

"Oops, sorry," I said.

She smiled at me over a bare shoulder. "I hope you don't mind. After all, you've seen me so often like this."

And she turned and moved with that languid sway of her hips that I knew so well to the table and shook a cigarette out of my pack.

She was like that. Because it had once been proper to be naked before me, she assumed it still was. I should have taken her in stride, ignored her; but I got sore because there were certain memories, all focused on the way she was now, that didn't do me any good to be revived.

I said, "You're wasting it on me, Gale. Why don't you try it on Nature Boy?"

She picked up an empty coffee cup and flung it at me. It sailed past my ear and smashed against the wall.

"You're aim hasn't improved," I told her.

She snatched up her clothes from the bed and stalked past me into the bathroom and slammed the door. I gathered up the remains of the cup. That little incident had been like a bit of our married life all over again, except that the last time she had thrown a cup at me it had had hot coffee in it.

She came out barefooted, but in skirt and blouse. While I poured coffee for both of us, she put on her stockings and shoes. Neither of us looked or sounded angry, but as we sat opposite each other at the table our conversation was limited to the care and feeding of Max. I think for the first time we disliked each other.

When she was ready to leave, I shut the dog in the bungalow to prevent him from following her car and walked out with her. Conrad Hickey, sketching busily, was facing us. Gale and I didn't kiss good-bye.

I stood watching her drive off, her face lovely behind the black veil, tendrils of her blonde hair waving in the breeze.

"Damn her!" I said aloud and returned to the bungalow.

Max had his long muzzle on extended paws and was looking up at me with liquid eyes. His absurd tail was a blur of friendliness. I brought him a saucer of water.

Chapter Two »»»

AT DAWN I STARTED out on my usual pre-breakfast walk. This time I had an enthusiastic companion—Max.

In previous walks, I had covered the outlying sections of the village, sticking to the roads that led past farmhouses and grazing fields and apple orchards. I had heard that there was nothing at all northeast, so I tried that now and found myself struggling against brush and fallen trees as I plodded along partly overgrown footpaths through scrub woods. I hadn't the soul of an explorer and it wasn't fun. For me, that is. Max had himself quite a time chasing whatever he heard or saw or smelled.

When I had gone about two miles, which was par for one way, I rested on a rock in a clearing and smoked my first cigarette of the day. That was when Max brought me the first bone.

He dropped it at my feet and gazed up at me with a pleased expression. It was a mighty big bone for such a small dog. I kicked it aside.

Yelping shrilly, he scurried off. A minute later he was brining me treasure to show that he had no resentment over having had his masters changed on him. He wanted to be patted.

I patted him.

I didn't straighten up at once. The smaller of the two bones held my gaze. It looked like a skeleton finger.

I picked it up. It had two joints like knuckles and bits of dried flesh adhered to it. I placed it next to my own fingers. It was shorter, but not much, and I have exceptionally big hands and long fingers.

Human? I didn't know. The only bones I had first-hand knowledge of were the bones of broiled T-bone steaks.

I examined the second bone. That could be a forearm from elbow joint to wrist. There was nothing but dirt on this one.

Probably from an animal. I dropped both bones and wondered if any animal had a bone in its paw with two joints and as big as that. Maybe a gorilla, but gorillas aren't common in New England.

"Max," I said. His tail wagged expectantly. "Max, where did you find these bones?" I waved the larger one under his nose. "Take me there."

He was eager to take me. He clamped the bone between his teeth and led me into brush that tore at my bare legs and at my shorts. Then he abandoned me in the midst of shoulder-high sumac.

"Max," I called.

He answered me. His shrill bark sounded in all directions. But he didn't appear. I fought my way through sumac and got nowhere except into more sumac. Eventually Max showed up and I followed him back to the clearing.

Both bones were gone. He had taken them away while I had been blundering in the sumac. When I asked him where they were, he got a shifty look in his eye and slunk away. Probably, after having brought them to me, he had decided that they could do him more good than me and had buried them.

I told myself that the bones may have come from an old Indian burial ground. But if so, would there still have been that flesh on the smaller? I told myself that very likely they weren't human. But what other animal had a bone like the small one with two joints? Maybe a bird, for all I knew, but no bird would have a bone as large as that other one. Finally I told myself that at any rate it wasn't my affair. I started back.

Bill Hickey was coming out of the house. When he saw me, he paused beside his car, on which was painted in vast letters STATE POLICE. He was a sergeant, beefy like most state troopers. At thirty-five or there-abouts, he was still a bachelor living with his parents.

"Going to be another scorcher today," he observed, taking a hitch at his gun belt and removing his Stetson.

I agreed that it would be and opened my mouth again to tell him about the bones Max had found. But I didn't. I'd be involved in whatever search there was, and if they were found they probably wouldn't mean anything and I'd appear somewhat ridiculous. Anyway, I'd come to North Set to be bothered by nothing and have nothing on my mind . . .

Bill Hickey drove off. I went into my bungalow and took a cold shower and made breakfast. I had twelve ounces of orange juice and hot cereal with plenty of sweet cream and three eggs and bacon and two glasses of milk. I was eating heartily again, for the first time in months.

Gale had been dead serious the day before when she had spoken about my ribs. I had never been husky. At six-feet-two, my top weight wasn't over a hundred and seventy pounds, but in March I had been twenty pounds under that, and I hadn't yet gained half of it back.

Dave Morrison, the Gothams' coach, held Gale responsible. She had liked the night life and had dragged me around with her when I should have been home in bed, and because, at the hot spots and parties, drinking liquor had been as natural as breathing, I'd done that too. On top of that, Dave had driven me too hard. There had been a tight race for second place, and then the play-offs. I was the play-maker and the only one who could hit consistently from outside, so he had given me little rest, I'd been murdered under the boards by the burly giants who infest the pro basketball game. And just about then our marriage had gone on the rocks. I'd been messed up inside and battered outside, and I'd ended each game so tired that I'd wanted to die.

The two months after the season had ended hadn't straightened me out, especially as far as hitting the bottle was concerned, but my placid existence here in North Set was doing the job. These mornings I got out of bed without that logy feeling and without my knees wobbling.

But this morning I was restless again. I had been since Gale's visit yesterday. I washed the breakfast dishes and made the bed and went outside with Max.

Conrad Hickey, as usual, was under the sugar maple with his easel and his colors. At the moment, he was working with pastels. As I approached, he quickly tacked a blank sheet of drawing paper on the easel. I said good morning.

"I see you have a dog," he declared with an exaggerated heartiness that implied a dog was a great thing to have. "Did that lovely lady who was here yesterday bring him?"

"Yes." The large sheet of drawing paper had only one thumbtack at the top; it flapped in the slight breeze. "What are you hiding there?"

"What in the world would I hide?" He beamed at Max,

who was using the tree trunk as a telephone pole. "That's a cute little fellow."

"Don't change the subject," I said. "You were sketching her yesterday from a distance. What have you done to her since then?"

Mr. Hickey sighed and yanked off the top sheet. Under it, four thumbtacks held another sheet firmly to the easel. It was a pastel drawing of Gale in the nude.

"She was quite inspiring," he apologized. "I did this from the sketches. It's practically finished."

I scowled at it. Her face was a pretty good likeness, but the important part was her figure, as it was in all his portraits of women. He hadn't had the advantage of seeing her in that bathing suit, for outside the bungalow she had worn either blouse and skirt or beach robe. He had made her body somewhat too buxom and her flesh was too lushly tinted, which was like gilding a lily, but all the same his imagination had captured the sensual essence of her.

"You disapprove, Harry," he said, anxiously peering up at my face. "I had planned to make an oil of her if the pastel worked out well." He became argumentative. "Didn't you tell me yesterday that she was nobody to you?"

"She was my wife until very recently."

"Oh." Gravely Mr. Hickey untacked the drawing. "Jessica calls me bawdy. That's all right: a certain amount of bawdiness is pleasant recreation for a man my age. But I'm afraid I've lost my sense of proportion."

He started to tear up the drawing.

"Wait a minute," I said. "Let me have it."

He rolled it up and handed it to me with a grin on his pixie face. "If you give me a couple of days, I can make an oil portrait for you to hang up over the fireplace."

"Go to hell!" I said, making myself smile as I said it.

Taking this portrait had been a damn fool thing to do, I told myself as I strode back to my bungalow. Gale shouldn't have come here, and, having come, she shouldn't have worn that bathing suit, and, having worn it, she shouldn't have removed it in the living room, casually and thoughtlessly showing me the only thing in our brief marriage that had been good, and what now, a man living alone, I missed.

In the bungalow I started to spread the drawing out on the table. I didn't quite unroll it. With a burst of good sense, I crumpled it and thrust it into the fireplace and put a match to it. I watched it burn.

Chapter Three »»»

THE BUSINESS SECTION of North Set consisted of Wellman's general store, with the post office as part of it, and the gas station across the road. Normally I walked the three-quarters of a mile for mail and supplies, but by eleven o'clock the sun was fierce; so I drove.

Mr. Wellman was sweeping the long, old-fashioned store porch. He was a thin, dour man, but when I ascended the two broad wooden steps he said with startling friendliness: "Morning, Mr. Wilde." I said good morning and went inside. Mrs. Wellman, fat as her husband was thin, beamed at me from the counter where she was waiting on a couple of kids. "How are you, Mr. Wilde?" I said I was fine and turned left to the post office window.

Polly Wellman was sorting mail. I watched her through the grille. She was very pleasant to watch. Comely was the word for her, without the implication of milk-fed buxomness. She was slimly and tightly put together, and I doubted that she was more than twenty. While she wasn't exactly scintillating, I'd found her restful company the two times I'd taken her out.

"Oh, hello, Harry." She had turned suddenly to see me

watch her, and she blushed.

At the moment, I approved of girls who blushed. I could not imagine anything being said or done to make Gale blush.

Polly brought my mail and my New York Times to the window. "Harry," she said, "are you busy tonight?"

"I'm never busy."

"Would you like to come to dinner then?"

I'd been a bachelor with a fair income too long not to be perpetually on guard. It was a condition unmarried girls and their parents invariably sought to abolish. Currently I was one again, and I recalled how her father, who had never before cracked a smile, had so cordially greeted me a couple of minutes before and how her mother had beamed at me. The jaws of the trap were opening. The young man, after two dates with the daughter, was being invited for a meal.

"I'm on a special training diet," I lied; "so I have to prepare my own meals."

"Tell me what you can eat and I'll cook it."

"It's too complicated." That didn't seem an adequate excuse; so I compromised. "But suppose I come around this evening and take you out?"

She accepted that with an open-mouthed smile. Her lips were soft and buttery. I had tasted them twice, briefly.

"At eight o'clock," she said.

I moved over to the counter and gave Mrs. Wellman my order, which consisted primarily of dog food. Mrs. Wellman didn't stop beaming at me. When I left, I wasn't sure I should have made any date at all with Polly.

Outside, in front of the store, a strange woman was stroking Max.

I hadn't brought him with me; he must have followed my car. He lay on his back, his legs stiff in the air and his stubby tail going and a look of ecstasy on his face as the crouching woman rubbed his gray-white belly.

"Evidently you like dogs," I said.

Black eyes tilted up to me. Nothing at all happened to her somewhat angular face. I didn't think it was a pretty face, but it was a face I could look at a long time. It remained expressionless. She straightened up, and in low-heeled shoes she came to my chin.

"Your dog?" she said, with a peculiar lack of interest considering she asked a question.

"Yes." Max righted himself. "Max," I said, "I'd like to introduce you to—"

"Mrs. Doane," she said, as if she didn't care whether I knew or not. She glanced down at the dog and then she smiled a little—so little that it was scarcely a flicker. "Max!" she muttered in a delayed echo and turned and walked across the road.

She wore a flaring skirt and a man's loose summer shirt, so that I could get no idea of her figure. Her bare legs, though, were very good. Her black hair was gathered in a severe bun. I wondered why I gave a damn about her figure and why I had maneuvered to learn her name.

Doane? Where had I heard it recently?

On the store porch, Mr. Wellman was leaning on the broom, watching Mrs. Doane getting into a battered station wagon across the road. And from the window in the post-office part of the store Polly was looking out at her too, with a kind of stiff-faced intensity.

Then I remembered the name. Nature Boy—Gale's companion at the swimming pool.

"Is she related to Dr. Doane?" I asked Mr. Wellman.

"Wife." He removed his pipe. "His latest one." The thin face became more dour than usual. "Anyway, she claims she's his wife."

Questions rose in my mind, but I didn't ask them. I didn't want to show special interest while Polly was at the window. But the interest was there. The station wagon crossed the road diagonally and passed within a few feet of me. She didn't as much as glance at me.

I waved good-bye to Polly and got into my car and held the door open for Max to join me.

At eight that evening, Polly was waiting for me on the dark store porch. She didn't care for my suggestion that we drive to Fort Able, where we could take in the movies or dance in a juke joint.

"It's a lovely night and there's a moon," she said. "Let's walk."

I parked the car and we strolled along the blacktop road. A breeze cut the heat. She looked trimly sweet in a snug cotton dress, and I felt her breast soft-firm as she hugged my arm.

"That flashy girlfriend of yours caused a lot of comment yesterday," she said, not quite viciously.

"That was no girlfriend. That was my ex-wife." And I told her just enough about Gale to get the facts straight.

Polly seemed relieved. That was a bad sign. I liked her, but not that much.

"They're still talking about her bathing suit," she said. "And how she carried on in public with Kenneth Doane."

"Is there anything you don't hear?"

"Well, everybody comes into Daddy's store and hangs around to gossip." She put her head back to give me a half-smile. "I noticed the way you were smitten by Mrs. Doane this morning."

"Me?" I said, more or less astonished. "I saw her for only a minute."

"What do you think of her?"

"In a minute? She's not particularly attractive and less friendly than most people in a small town."

"She's a queer one," Polly said, looking down at the ground. "They both are."

"Queer in what way?"

"Oh, let's not talk about anybody else."

I was willing. We turned up a narrower road, and as we walked my arm slipped as if by itself about her waist. At night I wasn't sure where we were and it didn't matter; she was taking me. We left that second road for a broad footpath through meadows and then we were at the bank of the creek, much narrower here than farther downstream at the pool. There were flat rocks on which to sit. We sat on one, with my arm still about her.

Moonlight glinted in her light-brown hair loose on her shoulders. Her face was small-boned and small-featured and very pretty. Kissing her then was the most natural thing in the world.

It wasn't like either of the two good-night kisses. Our bodies clung as well as our mouths.

Polly stroked my cheek and muttered, "Oh, honey!" and our hands and mouths kept seeking each other.

In the moonlight her skin had the translucent sheen of alabaster. She was compactly put together, with the tips of her perfectly rounded breasts impudently uptilted.

"Honey," she said hoarsely, "let's go to your bungalow."

For a moment I was very still.

"Don't be silly," I said.

"Why not?" The skin over her cheekbones was taut with

what she had stopped trying to control. Her body asserted itself, imposed itself. "You like me, don't you?"

It wasn't that simple. A man had to retain a certain amount of perspective. She was too young and probably too innocent; she was the local storekeeper's daughter; she would demand too much in return.

"Why not?" she said again, hugging my hand to the tingling softness of her. "We'll be so cozy there."

"We might be seen from the Hickey house."

"We can slip in."

"No!"

I snatched my hand from her and stood up and lit a cigarette and watched moonbeams dancing in the creek. I couldn't trust myself to go near her—anyway, not for a while. A bed in a bungalow wasn't required. Here on the grassy bank of the creek would do, and it would happen if I touched her again.

I'd had no right starting it. I could tell myself that I wouldn't have if Gale hadn't come to North Set yesterday and if Conrad Hickey hadn't let me see that pastel of Gale this morning and if for several months now I hadn't been in a lonely bed—but whatever the reason it was no excuse.

Some distance behind me Polly was quiet. I had a sense of her waiting there on that rock.

I thought: Well, why not? But I knew damn well why not. Gale maybe, if somehow it started again, or a woman like Mrs. Doane who—

I flung the cigarette from me; it hit the water, died and floated. Why the devil had Mrs. Doane entered my mind— a woman I had seen for only a minute and who wasn't especially pretty? I lit a fresh cigarette.

Polly spoke suddenly. "I hope, Harry, you didn't misunderstand," she said stiffly. "I didn't mean at all what you thought I meant by suggesting we go to your bungalow."

I turned to her. She sat rather primly, with her leg straight down and her skirt tight over her knees.

"I didn't think anything," I said.

"I'm glad you didn't. Of course, I'm not that kind of girl."

She was the kind of girl who would use a cliché when she had been turned down. No, I hadn't turned her down. I had avoided committing myself because she was marriageable and her father had been unusually cordial and her mother had beamed at me—because her quite desirable body was the bait in the trap.

We left the brook. We had been gone only an hour, but we started back to her house. Though her hand was again on my arm, it was there lightly; I couldn't feel her breast as we strolled, or her shoulder or hip. What I had done was best for her, and of course for me, but you can't sidestep a girl's passion and expect her to be grateful.

We were back on the pale strip of blacktop road when somebody approached us. At a distance of a hundred feet, his bulk and his close-cropped blond hair made him clearly recognizable. Gale's Nature Boy—Mrs. Doane's husband. Like myself, he wore a T-shirt, but my chest would never fill out one the way his did.

Polly and he exchanged nods when we were close enough. He ignored me. Maybe in that vague light he didn't recognize me as the man who had brought Gale to Twin Rock yesterday.

"Well, that's Mrs. Doane's husband," Polly said. "Isn't he a stunning man?"

"I suppose he makes women curl up and purr."

"Not me," she said. "You're more my type, Harry. And

you're very handsome, too, you know."

The Wellmans lived above their store. At the door we kissed good night. Now that we were in the shadow of her home, it was less dangerous. But it was ardent and I broke it up to ask her a question.

"What's Dr. Doane supposed to feed his wives?"

"His wives?" she said. "He has only one, of course. She's his second wife. What do you mean—feed them?"

"I've no idea what I mean. Let's try it this way. What does he feed them to?"

Polly turned a little so that her shoulder was against my chest. I couldn't see anything of her except her hair.

"So you heard the story?" she said. "It's about his first wife."

"Did I get the story right? Did he feed her to something?"

She pulled the door open. "It's only gossip." A shadowy smile crossed her lips. "You see, he keeps vicious dogs," she said almost gaily. "Good night, Harry."

Chapter Four »»»

MAX WOKE ME in the middle of the night. He was barking furiously as he raced about the room.

"Quiet!" I ordered.

That was five days after Gale had brought the dog to me, and he had learned to obey me. He spread himself out on the floor like a tiny black rug and whimpered. Perhaps somebody was outside. I lay listening. I heard stealthy movement or thought I did; if anything, it would be an animal.

I fell asleep.

What woke me next time was a heavy thumping on the floor. I sat up in bed. Max was growling far back in his throat, trying to mute his voice for fear of my displeasure and not quite succeeding. The thumping was repeated—a thumping followed by clawing at the door.

"Who's there?" I called.

Silence then. I felt sweat on my brow.

The door was unlocked. Anybody who wanted to come in could have simply opened it. Anybody human.

I got out of bed and looked through the window beside the door. In what light remained from a dying moon, I saw an enormous form slink away. On the driveway a smaller shape, less exaggerated by shadows, squatted motionless on its haunches.

Dogs. Only dogs. I returned to bed.

Max had crawled under my bed. He didn't stop whimpering. And suddenly I thought of what Polly Wellman had told me—or at any rate, hinted at—about Dr. Doane's dogs.

Had they been sent here to get me?

I regretted not having locked the door when I had been out of bed. I began to worry about the windows. They were all wide open, though screened. I thought of locking the door and closing the windows, but I knew I wouldn't. That act would be too much concession to preposterous worrying.

I turned over on my side and tried to sleep, but now bones popped into my mind. The two bones Max had found several mornings ago several miles from here. Dogs could have picked them clean of flesh.

Suppose some monstrous, ravenous dogs got into the bungalow to feed. Afterward they'd worry whatever was left until some bones, like a forearm or a finger, came off from the rest, and each would run off with what it had and maybe bury it and dig it up later—but the bone would be the thing, a dog and his bone.

More fantasy, this time developing into a half-waking nightmare. I roused myself fully, went into the kitchen for a drink of water. I looked through windows on all four sides of the bungalow and saw nothing. Maybe they'd never been here; maybe I'd had a bad dream inspired by two disconnected things that had happened several days ago, the finding of two bones and a silly bit of gossip.

After that I slept soundly.

But in the morning they were back, with reinforcements. I saw them right after I got out of bed, when I opened the door for Max to go out. They made for him. He ran a few steps toward them, yelped, and scooted back into the bungalow. I slammed the door.

I almost decided to call off my pre-breakfast walk. But I'd never been afraid of dogs; I wouldn't begin now. I dressed. Max was eagerly pawing the door, but when I went through it he hesitated.

Only for a moment, though. The morning walks with me had become the high spot of his existence; the lure was too great. He stayed close to me, growling viciously, for such a small thing, when the dogs converged toward him.

"Scat!" I said. "Beat it!"

They obeyed to the extent of moving slowly and with dignity and then settling themselves down to watch us. There were five of them now. The largest was a mean-looking German shepherd, probably the one who had tried to batter my door down during the night. I wouldn't want to meet him on a dark night if he objected to me. Another was a handsome red setter, and the others, all considerably larger than Max, were breeds I didn't recognize, or no particular breed. I knew little about dogs except that too many were enough.

I walked and Max walked and they walked. I picked up a handful of stones and now and then tossed one, without malice and generally without accuracy. That, at any rate, kept them from swarming over us. After a while, I picked up a sturdy branch; this impressed them more than the stones. Also, it was a weapon of sorts if I should need one.

I walked north to the clearing beside the impassable sumac, where the other morning Max had found the bones.

I said: "Max, go find your bones. Dig them up where you buried them. Go find others. Bones, Max."

I spoke as if I were trying to explain something to a mental defective, and Max gave me the response I deserved. He looked up at me and wagged his stubby tail and didn't stir.

All the same, it might have worked if it hadn't been for our escorts. A dog would return to his buried bones; he might have dug them up from wherever he had buried them. But not this morning when he was afraid to leave me for a moment, when all about us, in the brush, in the woods, in the sumac, shapes slunk and prowled, sometimes fighting among themselves, but always near where we were.

And the shapes followed us home, and as I ate breakfast I saw them from the window. There were six now, standing, lying, squatting on the driveway and the small patch of grass, now and then playing together with the blatant indecency of canines, never going completely away.

An hour after breakfast I drove to Twin Rock for a swim. Max, for once, had no desire to go with me; he had crawled under the bed and stayed there, as if hiding. And when I returned at noon, more dogs had joined the vigil—dogs of every size, breed, and color. I had to plow through them from car to bungalow, and, before I reached the door, I saw Jessica Hickey come toward me from the house.

She wore blue denim slacks and a frilly blouse, and her forthright stride looked all wrong for a small, gray-haired woman. The inevitable cigarette was in the corner of her mouth.

"I see you're besieged," she said cheerfully.

"You're telling me! What are they after?"

"These are all males. What are males of any species after? Your dog's in heat."

"That occurred to me, but it's impossible. Max is a—" I stopped. "Are you sure?"

"I can make sure," she said.

We entered the bungalow. Max came out from under the bed when I called. He was anxious for affection, but Mrs. Hickey didn't waste time patting him. Efficiently she turned him over on his back and held him pinned to the floor.

"Of course," she said. "Didn't you notice?"

"I never paid attention. But look. If Max is in heat, would he—I mean she—be so antagonistic toward those males?"

"She's only in the first stage," Mrs. Hickey said.

"How long will her suitors be hanging around?"

"Until she's over it. Three weeks, about. I doubt that all the male dogs in the neighborhood have arrived yet."

"My God, I'm not going through three weeks of this!"

"Either that or get rid of her. That's why people prefer males. They live their love lives away from home." She smiled. "No doubt that's one reason most people would rather have sons."

"Do you have to compare dogs with humans?"

"There's not much difference when it comes to sex." Mrs. Hickey tossed her cigarette into the fireplace and left.

I put in a phone call to Gale in New York. It was only a few minutes after twelve; if she was keeping to her usual routine, she would still be in bed. But there was no answer.

In the afternoon I drove to Fort Able for meat and other supplies Wellman's didn't sell. It was an excuse to get away from the bungalow. When I returned, I counted eleven. They greeted me joyously, as if I had come to let them in and hand them sex on a platter. The big shepherd would have followed me in if I hadn't kicked him none too gently in the nose.

I kept trying Gale's number. It was close to six o'clock before I heard her voice.

"Gale, prepare yourself for a shock. Max turns out to be

a girl."

"Why, of course," her voice came blithely over the wire. "What did you think he was?"

"He!" I didn't quite choke. "He! I've been brought up to assume that a 'he' is a male."

"That's just a way of talking, silly. People call all dogs 'he' just as they call all cats 'she.'"

"All right," I said. "But Max? Since when is Max a feminine name?"

"His name is really Maxine. I call him Max for short."

I closed my eyes.

"Hair-y, are you there?" she said.

"I'm here," I said. "So are a dozen sex-starved hounds, all eager to become the father of her children."

"No! Max is only ten months old."

"She precocious. I've no intention of being swamped by her boyfriends for the next three weeks. I'm driving to New York tonight and returning her to you."

"Hair-y, you can't. The building superintendent—"

"I can and will."

"Why don't you take Max to a dog kennel? I hear people leave them there till they get over it."

For once she had come up with a sound idea. "All right," I conceded.

"You're a sweet man, darling."

I said good-bye and hung up and went out. This time I counted nine. Some must have gone home for dinner. A few followed me hopefully to the Hickey house, as if I might have Max—that is, Maxine—tucked in my pocket.

The three Hickeys were eating at the kitchen table. I apologized for breaking in on their meal and asked Bill Hickey, who as a state trooper would know, where the nearest dog kennel was.

"There used to be one over in Gill Valley," he said, "but I heard they closed, and anyway it's a good forty miles."

"What about Doane?" Mr. Hickey suggested. "He boarded Sara Blair's terrier when she went to California, and he has four or five of his own."

"Do you mean Dr. Doane?" I asked.

"That's right," Mr. Hickey said. "The veterinarian. Do you know him?"

"I've seen him, but I didn't know he was an animal doctor. I thought he was an M.D."

Mrs. Hickey sniffed. "I wouldn't trust him with a pet mouse, let alone a human being."

"Don't talk like that, Jessica," Mr. Hickey chided her gently. "Just because—" He broke a roll in two. "The local farmers swear by him. They say he's wonderful with animals. He'll take your dog, Harry, and help us get some peace around here."

"Peace?" Bill echoed in a whisper, and he dipped his face to the soup bowl.

His parents looked at him and they too resumed eating, and I had a feeling that I had intruded on something very personal.

I broke the silence to ask how to get to Doane's house. Mr. Hickey told me that it was a couple of miles from here, at the end of a tar road called Birch Lane. I couldn't miss it, he said.

And that was how I came to go there.

Chapter Five »»»

FIRST THERE was the sound that had become depressingly familiar: the frenzied barking of dogs. They had been roused by my approaching car. All I saw was the crumpling tar road, worse even than most roads in North Set, and brush-covered fields. Nobody seemed to live this far out. Then I rounded a curve and there on my left were two buildings.

One was a two-story frame house, loaded with gables and gingerbread. Once it had been white, but not for many years; its weathered coat was like flaky ash. Across a hundred feet of bare, hard ground on which nothing grew stood a rambling barn in even worse shape—its color a kind of pale pink where it had once been vigorous red and its roof partially open to the wind and rain.

In spite of the dogs and the fact that the road ended here, I didn't quite believe this could be the place until I noticed nailed to the trunk of a scrawny roadside tree a frayed board announcing in surprisingly neat block letters: KENNETH S. DOANE, VETERINARIAN. I swung the car in, and at once three lunging dogs tried to assault it.

They were all big and looked and sounded vicious, and one was the already familiar German shepherd. There was another shepherd, a trifle smaller, and a chow with a mean face. Those two hadn't been among the host outside my bungalow; I guessed they must be females if they had stayed away, and later I learned I was right. Maxine rose up at the car window and yelped back at them in her shrill voice. I stopped the car between the house and the barn and waited in bedlam, not daring to get out. I honked the horn.

Mrs. Doane appeared on the porch and stopped at the head of sagging, peeling wooden steps and called: "Yes?"

"Is Dr. Doane in?" I shouted above the uproar.

"No."

She didn't come down from the porch. While the dogs kept up their clamor, she stood there in a gingham dress with a broad, square bodice and her black hair knotted in. back of her head and her angular face completely static and her black eyes, without anything in them, fixed on my face in the car window.

"Look," I yelled. "What will these dogs do to me if I get out of the car?"

She didn't tell me, but she did descend the porch steps. "Down," she said quietly to the dogs.

The effect was miraculous. Immediately they subsided. They sensed her next command, or perhaps she made a gesture that escaped me. They slunk to the barn and spread themselves out in front of the broad barn door, abruptly docile, even the sex-hungry shepherd. Maxine tossed one more yelp of defiance at them and dropped down to the seat, looking as smug as if she had put them to rout.

"They certainly obey you," I observed, making conversation.

"I taught them to," Mrs. Doane said in that colorless voice of hers. She remained where she was, some ten feet from the car, not coming nearer, not asking me what I wanted.

I gathered Maxine up in my arms and went out to Mrs. Doane. I said: "Now I know why you smiled the other morning when I told you the dog's name was Max. I found out this morning how wrong I was about her sex. It turns out her name is really Maxine and she's in heat."

"So that's where King and Major have been all day."

"That's right," I said. "They and a dozen others."

She laid a hand on Maxine's head and stroked her as I held her. The hand was brown and strong-looking and without nail polish. Her throat was brown, too, richly smooth, and so was the area of skin visible at the deep square bodice of the gingham dress. I found my gaze drawn there as if by itself. When I realized I was beginning to stare, I raised my eyes to her black hair.

Mrs. Doane seemed to be completely unaware of me except as a fixture holding a dog. Saying nothing, she continued to pat Maxine. She didn't make it easy for me to talk to her.

"The males started coming last night," I said, "and I've already had too much. I heard that you—that Dr. Doane would board . . ."

"He's not here."

"Well, does he board dogs?"

"I can't tell you. He's not here."

"Do you expect him soon?" I persisted. "Can I wait?"

"If you want to."

Her hand never left Maxine. It was her left hand and there was a simple gold band on the third finger. A shoddy ring, like everything else in the place—except the woman, and about her I knew nothing. Maxine was the reason or excuse or whatever else it may have been for our standing so close together, and somehow I felt that we were even closer as I watched that brown hand move gently over the thick black fur, almost touching my arm and chest as it stroked. There was none of the random conversation two waiting strangers exchanged, nothing at all to ease a situation that was beginning to make me shiver.

Then she raised her head and said: "He's coming."

I heard a car puffing and squeaking. She stepped away, putting distance between us—not hurrying, but evidently not wanting whoever was arriving to find us close together.

The battered station wagon turned in from the road. It pulled up next to my coupe, and Kenneth Doane climbed out.

"Hello," he said to me. Then his pale eyes lighted on Maxine and softened. "What have we here?"

I explained.

"Of course we'll take care of you, girl," he told Maxine affectionately and reached for her.

She knew a friend when she saw one. Contentedly, she snuggled in the crook of his brawny arm. "Mostly spitz," he observed professionally. "A bit of water spaniel and maybe terrier."

"Quite an impressive ancestry," I said.

He made no comment. Neither of the Doanes was exactly the garrulous type. He bore Maxine off to a wire-fence paddock beside the barn. He opened a gate and whistled and the dogs rose from the barn door and raced through the gate.

There were four of them now. I recognized the newcomer—the red setter that had been still hanging around my bungalow when I had driven off. He, too, had come home for dinner, and I could see them tearing away at it in the paddock as Doane strode on with Maxine.

Mrs. Doane hadn't stirred. Her hands were clasped. I thought of commenting on the weather, anything to break the silence. Instead I moved toward the paddock, wanting to see what Maxine's temporary home would be like.

It was at the far end of the paddock—a quite small, disreputable-looking shack, something like a squat outhouse. Gale wouldn't have been happy about it.

Then I saw what the dogs were eating. Savagely they tore at raw, red meat attached to something pretty big. Some of it was already down to bone stripped clean-bone that was a terrible white under the sinking sun.

"It's part of a horse," Mrs. Doane said. She had come up beside me. "My husband had to destroy a farmer's horse that had hurt itself in some way and he bought the carcass cheap."

"Yes, of course," I muttered.

What else could the meat have been?

All the same, I turned away, slightly sickened for no reason I could understand. And I felt the back of her hand against my arm.

It was nothing. She had turned at the same time and her hand had brushed my arm. It was nothing, but I didn't move my arm away and her hand didn't move either, and for a long moment, stretching out almost unendurably, that small contact held, and I felt it send out radiations down to my stomach, gripping it, and up to my throat, constricting it. Then she had flowed away from me and I saw her husband coming back across the paddock without Maxine.

He made sure the gate was closed behind him. A hundred feet away in the shack I heard Maxine barking in distress.

"I hate to shut up any animal," he told me. "I'll let her have a run every day."

"Won't all the male dogs come here now?"

"No. Mine will keep them away. What's her name?"

"Maxine."

He didn't ask for my name. Perhaps he didn't consider a man as important as an animal. He had shown enough interest in Gale at Twin Rock, however, and maybe she had told him who I was.

Side by side we walked to my car, both of us the same height, but I felt anemic next to him. Mrs. Doane was ahead of us. Without saying good-bye, without even a backward glance at me, she went into the house.

At my car I asked him what I owed him. He said five dollars a week. That was very reasonable.

As I took out my wallet, he shuffled a foot like an embarrassed school-boy and muttered: "Could you pay me three weeks in advance? Of course you don't have to, but well . . ."

"Glad to."

But when he had the money, he didn't thank me. Without counting the bills, he stuffed them into his pants pocket and wandered away. Just like that. You not only didn't get more than the absolute minimum of conversation from the Doanes; you didn't even get good-byes.

When I was back on the blacktop road, I stopped the car to draw in my breath and light a cigarette. It was as if I needed a motionless period away from everything to orient myself. My hand shook a little and something jittered in the pit of my stomach. It had never been anything like this before and with so little reason.

I didn't know if she was beautiful or not. I didn't remember, and when I had been with her I hadn't thought in terms of beauty. I'd had no such doubts with Gale's splendid good looks or with Polly Wellman's sweet prettiness or with any other woman. Maybe she was even ugly with that angular, static face, and I had never known a woman more aloof.

Except when her hand had been against my arm lightly and yet remaining there—a hand with a wedding ring on it.

I drove on.

Chapter Six »»»

NEXT DAY I had lunch with Mr. and Mrs. Hickey in their kitchen, old-fashioned in its bigness and brightness and modern with its gleaming gadgets. Over the tuna-fish salad, I brought the conversation around to the Doanes.

"Quite a place," I said.

"Place or woman?" Mr. Hickey asked with his impish smile.

"Place and woman and man and dogs. The whole setup is slightly weird. No wonder people make up fantastic stories."

Mrs. Hickey put down her fork. "What makes you think they're fantastic?"

"Actually all I've heard was something vague about his former wife and those dogs. Of course there can't be anything in it."

"How do you know there can't?" she demanded pugnaciously, as if I were challenging a cherished local tradition.

"Well, is there?"

"I've no idea," she said crisply and resumed eating.

Mr. Hickey grinned. "Let's stop being devious, Harry. You're fishing for the story of Kenneth Doane and his women, and why not? Sticking one's nose into other people's business is the essence of good conversation. Alice Barton was his first wife. She was a teacher in the district school— an attractive, refined, quiet girl who never had much to say."

"Seems Doane doesn't care for talkative women," I commented.

"You found the current Mrs. Doane like that too, eh? Well, yes. His first wife, Alice Barton, wasn't a native. She came from the other end of the state. No parents living, she told me, more or less alone in the world. I was a member of the School Board at the time, and besides, she used to . . ."

He stopped speaking. There was a look of pain in Mrs. Hickey's strong face.

"Anyway," he resumed, "one summer—four years ago, as I recall—Alice went off on her summer vacation and came back a week before school opened with Kenneth Doane and a wedding ring. Nobody knew a thing about him except that he was a licensed veterinarian. He had no money. The story is that it was with her savings that they made the down payment on the old Leonard place. You've seen it. It was a ruin when they bought it, and it still is. About all they did to it was put in plumbing and a heating system."

"Evidently he's still poor," I said. "Doesn't being a veterinarian pay around here?"

"Not well, and they say he's not very bright about money. Or about anything else, if you ask me. Alice, of course, continued to teach after her marriage. She had to, though there was also the fact that she was very fond of teaching."

"I still don't understand why a sensible and intelligent girl like her married a dull and shiftless man like him," Mrs. Hickey put in.

"Jessica, my dear, all women aren't like you, preferring a husband with brains and character instead of good looks.

You must admit he's quite a hunk of man. Well, the following summer—that was two years after they were married—they shut up the house and left. Just like that. No good-byes to anybody. One day they closed down the house and were gone. With the dogs, of course. They must have piled the four monsters into that station wagon, and the two of them—"

"The two?" Mrs. Hickey said. "How do you know? Nobody saw them leave."

"No, nobody saw them leave," he conceded. "Nobody knew where they went. Nobody again saw Alice or heard of her. The school term opened and never a word from her that she wasn't coming back to teach. You can make any kind of old wives' tale of that you wish, and idle gossips certainly did. Anyway, some eight months later—a year ago last spring that was—Kenneth Doane was suddenly back in his house. He and the dogs and another woman with another wedding ring. The present Mrs. Doane. Not a word of explanation to anybody. He was simply back, taking up where he had left off, except with a different wife."

I said: "No doubt that's when the story that he had murdered his first wife started."

"Wasn't it inevitable? Given that setup and that place, which you've aptly described as weird, people's imaginations will work overtime. And given those vicious dogs, why not make the story gruesome while you're at it?"

"Is the present Mrs. Doane a local girl?"

"Humph!" Mrs. Hickey snorted. "She came up to North Set with that no-good George Wellman."

"Any relative to Polly Wellman?"

Mr. Hickey answered that. "Her brother. A slick article. I disliked him as a boy. Too conniving. Some years ago he moved to New York, where he's a gambler, I hear. Perhaps you've heard of him, Harry, or know him. I understand that there is a lot of gambling on basketball games."

"The law says I'm not supposed to even say hello to a gambler."

"A good law. Where are we? Oh, yes—the present Mrs. Doane hadn't been a complete stranger to North Set. When Doane and Alice were still living here, she had spent several hours here with George Wellman. You can speculate on the relationship between her and George at the time, but I prefer to leave scandal to clean-minded women like my wife."

"Your sarcasm doesn't faze me," Mrs. Hickey snapped. "Didn't she and George drive up from New York together? And they didn't spend a few hours. They spent a night."

"Woman," he said, "you can reach any conclusion you desire from basically innocent facts. They spent that day and night with George's family, and it's undeniable that she slept with his sister Polly." He turned his head to me. "This, of course, was about a year before she returned to North Set as the second Mrs. Doane. The prevailing theory is that she saw that manly torso of his and fell for him in a split second, and that Doane reciprocated."

"What did he see in her?" Mrs. Hickey voiced the age-old complaint. "Alice was so much prettier and nicer than that wooden-faced brunette."

He smiled tolerantly. "That's a woman's opinion, which doesn't count because Doane happens to be a man. Men don't always prefer women who are merely pretty and nice. Well, they must have met that night because she was not again seen in North Set until, as I said, about a year later he returned without Alice and with the present Mrs. Doane as his wife."

"Wait," I said. "Is he supposed to have murdered Alice before or after he left North Set?"

"It's not supposition," he corrected me. "It's talk, and as a lawyer I can tell you there's a thumping difference between fact and talk. But if you grant the assumption, he would have fed her to his dogs, or whatever he did with her, just before he left. That's why my wife makes such a point of the fact that nobody saw him when he drove off. Alice may have been with him or not, for all anybody knows."

I realized then that I would have to make another and more thorough search for the bones Maxine had found.

"But shouldn't the police have looked into Alice's disappearance as a matter of routine?" I said. "Your son Bill must have known her, must have heard the stories, and he's a state police sergeant."

Abruptly Mrs. Hickey rose and went to the electric range.

"Bill did look into it," Mr. Hickey said as he picked at what remained of his salad. "He questioned Doane, and Doane said that he and Alice had been divorced in Florida."

Mrs. Hickey returned to the table with the coffee pot. A cigarette now dangled from the corner of her mouth. "And Bill believed him," she said scornfully.

"What would you have, woman?" her husband said. "Bill isn't paid to devote his time to every wild tale inspired by wagging tongues. He asked Doane and received a reasonable answer. Pass the sugar, Harry."

We drank coffee in silence. Then, trying to sound casual, I asked: "By the way, what's the present Mrs. Doane's first name?"

"I'm sure I never heard it," Mrs. Hickey replied. "Nobody in town is familiar enough with her to call her anything but Mrs. Doane. But ask my husband." Her mouth tightened.

"He painted her picture."

"To me, Jessica, she was and is also strictly Mrs. Doane." He addressed me. "I asked her to pose for me and she consented, I did an oil of her and presented it to her. No, Harry, I do not know her first name."

After lunch, Conrad Hickey invited me up to his studio. It had once been the attic; the entire north half of the roof had been torn out and replaced with sloping glass. It seemed ideal, but he complained that it was hot in summer and cold in winter and that, anyway, he preferred painting outdoors.

"I want to show you something," he said. He took out keys and unlocked a built-in cabinet, but he didn't open the door right away. His manner had become unusually grave for him. "Before I do, Harry, understand this. I don't make a practice of doing those imaginative nudes of real women. Perhaps I have a latent sense of decency. There were, however, two exceptions. One you know: the pastel I did the other morning of your ex-wife. I couldn't resist, and I'm not going to apologize again."

"That's all right," I said. "Gale feels the same way about clothes. She generally wears the minimum the law allows." I drew cigarette smoke into my lungs. "I'm guessing that the other exception is Mrs. Doane."

"Yes."

He reached into the cabinet and brought out a fairly large mounted canvas. He placed it against the wall am stepped out of the way.

She wasn't merely nude. She was naked. Nothing I had seen of his had been as good and as true and, in a way, as shocking.

"You—" I had to stop to clear my throat. "Don't tell me she posed for you like that!"

"Hardly. All four sittings were on her porch and her husband was usually around. She wore a rather form fitting and revealing evening gown, but respectable enough. You'll find the original painting in her house, if you ever enter it, and I'm afraid you will. Before I presented it to her, I made this copy up here. What do you think of it?"

I made an effort to sound objective. "You drew her a bit—well, fleshier than she is."

"Do you already know, Harry?"

I flushed angrily. "Look, I don't have to stand for you being nasty."

"I'm sorry. I wouldn't know either and probably you're right that I made her too fleshy, but I did it on purpose. I wasn't striving for a reproduction; I was trying to say something. She could be thin as a rail, and she would still give the impression of fleshiness. A woman of flesh. Isn't that the way she affected you?"

"I don't know," I lied.

"And the face. When I started to paint the original portrait, I thought her face was wooden, expressionless. But I soon discovered how wrong I was. An artist must look beneath the surface. It's a slumberous face—a face that waits in repose to be periodically awakened. Do you understand what I'm saying?"

I couldn't breathe while I looked at the painting. I turned away.

"Did you ever watch a praying mantis?" he went on. "How very still, merging with the vegetation, waiting with deathless patience, then pouncing. And you must have heard how the female praying mantis devours her mate during the very act of sex." His voice lowered. "Harry, don't let her devour you."

"What?" I stared at him as he stood before me, slight and with his pinched face so solemn that there was nothing of the pixie left in it. "What the devil are you saying?"

"I like you, Harry. Don't let her devour you."

"You're crazy. I hardly know her."

"You hardly know her, but for the first time since you've been here you've consented to have a meal with us so that you could pump us about her."

"I haven't wanted to get into the habit of imposing on Mrs. Hickey."

"But today that didn't matter because you'd been at the Doane house last evening and had to know more about her. And you were anxious to learn her first name."

I said stiffly, "I'm sorry I accepted your hospitality. It won't happen again."

"Don't be a blathering idiot, Harry. We're the same kind of men. The difference is that I'm so much older and she's unavailable; so my mind isn't clouded by her." He scowled at the picture. "I'm not much of an artist. Probably I didn't get into it what I intended to. But you ought to see a little of it. Not evil. I don't think that's it. A man-eating beast isn't any more evil than a beast-eating man. But they're dangerous to each other. Look at her, Harry. Don't you see the menace of her?"

I looked again and saw the portrait of a woman's body in rich, expressive oils—a body and face beautiful or not, it didn't matter, the vividly revealed woman who yesterday had lightly touched my arm with the back of her hand and had charged me with something that was beyond restlessness.

I said: "All I see is that you have no right to paint such a picture without the woman's consent and then go showing it around."

"Only you and I know it exists." He carried the painting back to the cabinet. "And perhaps I shouldn't have shown it to you."

Why had he? Not for the reason he had stated—to discourage desire. He would know that it was bound to have the opposite effect.

"But I hope it will put you on guard," he was saying as he turned from the cabinet.

He knew better than that. The painting was a lure, not a warning.

"On guard against what?" I said obstinately.

He looked at me for a long time, and I couldn't meet his gaze. "We men," he said softly, "we like to feel superior to those male dogs who hung around outside your bungalow. But are we?"

I was seething with fury. "Who the hell appointed you the guardian of my morals? For that matter, yours can stand looking into."

"Isn't that the truth?" he said cheerfully. "Let's not quarrel. No woman is worth it, particularly at my age. A friend sent me a bottle of Portuguese brandy. I haven't opened it yet. Help me sample it."

I followed him downstairs. Why, I asked myself, was he subtly and diabolically trying to drive me into her arms? That question assumed that he wanted to and that she would have me. He wasn't a stupid man, not realizing what he was doing. He was one of the cleverest men I knew.

We were in the living room. He poured brandy and we raised our glasses.

"To Maxine's suitors," he toasted impishly, "our understanding and sympathy."

I hesitated with the glass halfway to my mouth. He watched me with his grin broadening, as if wondering if I would throw the brandy in his face. I drank it down and left.

Chapter Seven »»»

THE STATION WAGON passed me the following afternoon when I was trudging home with the mail. I could recognize it from a distance by the squeak and rattle, by its weathered and unpainted appearance—like their house and their barn —and by the front bumper askew.

As I stepped to the side of the road, I wondered with an annoying constriction in my chest if she was in it and alone and if she would stop to speak to me.

Then it was rolling by, not fast because nothing either of the Doanes did would be hurried, and for an instant Kenneth Doane and I looked at each other. His square jaw bobbed vaguely in a nod, and he was probably past before I returned it.

She wasn't with him.

I stood watching the wobbling tail of the station wagon. Wellman's store was still in sight. Doane didn't stop there, which meant he was going past the village, to Fort Able or to make a professional call. He wouldn't be likely to return home very soon.

I walked on. The sun baked me as it baked the road, but,

even so, I was sweating more than I should have. I didn't go into my bungalow. I stopped beside my car, watching Mr. Hickey painting under the maple without quite seeing him. Then I tossed my mail on the car seat and got behind the wheel and backed out of the driveway.

Once, on the way, I said to myself: Don't be a damn fool. But that didn't make me stop and go back.

The dogs greeted me. They were less vociferous than two days ago, probably because this time I didn't have Maxine with me, but they looked and acted frightening enough. I stepped out among them, saying, "Down!" and at least they didn't get closer to me. Though they looked as if they would have liked to, particularly that male shepherd.

Exactly as two days ago, Mrs. Doane came out on the porch and said impassively, "Yes?"

She wore the same flaring skirt and loose-fitting man's shirt as the first time I had seen her, outside Wellman's store. She struck me, with a kind of shock, as considerably less than alluring. The angular lines of her face were harsh, and the way she stood there gave an effect of complete rejection.

I went to her, with the clamoring dogs following.

"Down!" she ordered.

Instantly they shut up and let me alone, and in the silence I heard Maxine's shrill bark in the distant shack.

I stood at the foot of the porch steps and looked up at Mrs. Doane. "I stopped by to see how my dog is getting on."

"My husband isn't here."

"Well, can't you tell me?"

"She's all right."

A long moment of silence. Then I said, "Can I see her?"

"Come back when my husband is here."

And that was all. I should have known that there couldn't even be conversation with her. What had I expected?

"Thanks," I said and started back to my car.

My hand was on the door handle when I heard her voice.

"Would you like a drink?"

I turned. She hadn't stirred. Her tone had been neither friendly nor unfriendly—simply flat and colorless.

"Why, sure," I said.

"I have only water. We don't drink anything stronger."

"I prefer water in this weather."

She didn't wait for me. She was already in the house when I reached the porch. I pulled open a sagging screen door and entered a living room, dim because of the porch roof in front and trees close to the side windows. The furniture was moth-eaten mohair, looking as old as the house, and there was a threadbare rug.

She was standing across the room, facing me with strong brown hands clasped, and I could feel the stillness of her. A slumberous woman, Mr. Hickey had said, but I thought rather a woman who kept herself remote and indrawn.

She had invited me in here, but that meant nothing. Anyone would be polite enough to offer a man water on a hot day.

I glanced about for the fireplace; above it, of course, hung the painting. It was in an ornate discolored gilt frame which must have been dug out of an attic. The face in this painting was softer than in the copy Mr. Hickey had shown me yesterday, softer than the face watching me. He had stressed delicate tones and shading, prettifying it as if to please the sitter. As for the figure—well, in this painting it was clad in a white evening gown that left fine brown shoulders and the upper slopes of her bosom bared; by contrast, it had no life to it.

This was, after all, only a portrait done by a fairly competent amateur. The same couldn't be said of the one locked in a cabinet in Mr. Hickey's studio.

"Conrad Hickey painted it," she said. "Do you like it?"

"It doesn't do you justice."

"Oh, but it flatters me. I'm not as pretty."

That was it—she was not as pretty. She was something more than pretty or different from pretty—something I had no word as yet to describe.

Then I realized that we had exchanged personal words. She had discussed herself as a woman. It was like being introduced.

She said, "Come into the kitchen," and went through a door. I followed.

The kitchen needed paint and the sink was chipped and two of three wooden chairs had rungs missing. I felt a mounting distaste for the place that reached out and included her. If her husband was too shiftless to wield a paint brush and a hammer, she might have tried it.

She filled a glass at the tap and handed it to me. Our fingers brushed. She stepped back into a splash of sunlight pouring through an unobstructed window and her dark eyes watched me drink.

"You're tall," she said.

But there was no animation, almost no interest—a flat statement of fact as if I were some kind of animal to be appraised.

"So is your husband," I said dryly. "And he's bigger and handsomer."

At last her eyes showed something, a momentary flash like two sparks deep in the black pupils.

"I don't like you," she said.

Grinning, I finished the water. We were becoming practically intimate.

I started to place the empty glass on the table. She took it from me and carried it to the sink and said without turning: "I was sure you would come back."

"Are you glad I did?"

"Yes." She faced me, her hands held spread on either side of the sink apron as she stood against it. "I was afraid you'd come when my husband was here. You mustn't ever, even to see your dog."

"What would he do if he found me here?"

"Kill you perhaps," she said negligently, as if it would be a small matter.

I felt my mouth twist. Words came out by themselves. "And then what—feed me to those dogs outside?"

She was stiller than the sink behind her.

"Now I like you even less," she said petulantly—the first time her voice had carried any sort of emotion.

So there we were, facing each other, understanding each other and what each wanted, but no closer together in any way. I had ruined it by perversely opening my big mouth. Maybe subconsciously I had wanted to ruin it.

She straightened up against the sink. "Aren't you going to kiss me?" she said a trifle impatiently.

I went to her. I put my hands on her shoulders. Under the shirt her flesh was warm and smooth. She didn't tilt back her head. She seized my upper arms, her nails digging in, and propelled herself up along my body, and I felt her clenched teeth bruise my lips.

It was less a kiss than an assault, an explosion.

She quivered against me, clinging with hands and mouth,

and then suddenly she subsided and might have fallen if I hadn't held her. Her face was on my chest and her hair against my mouth. She didn't stop trembling.

"I can't keep calling you Mrs. Doane," I said. "What's your first name?"

"Lela."

"Lela," I repeated, tasting it. "My name's Harry Wilde."

"Yes, I know. Kiss me once more."

This one was different. Her mouth opened and melted under mine and her body was limp against me. It lasted a long time.

"Now do you like me any better?" I said when we were apart and I was lighting a cigarette.

"What has that to do with it?"

I would have laughed if she had been anybody else. She had uttered a basic truth—for me and for herself. No, we did not even have to like each other.

She was completely composed as she had not been during those two kisses. I watched her tuck a loose strand of black hair back into her bun, and I thought: What now?

I said it aloud. "What now, Lela?"

"You'll have to leave at once."

"Should I phone you?"

"No. Don't ever do that."

"I guess you're right. You phone me. I live in the Hickey bungalow."

"I know. But we mustn't phone each other. They're all party lines; people might listen in. I'll get in touch with you."

"All right." I took the cigarette from my mouth and moved to kiss her.

She held me off with a hand and averted her face.

"Don't! I couldn't stand it again without—" She turned

her back. "Go! Hurry!"

I was at the kitchen door before I thought of saying good-bye. "Good-by, Lela. I'll be seeing you soon, then?"

"Yes."

"How soon?"

"I don't know."

I went then. I paused on the porch. My throat was dry. I drew cigarette smoke past it.

There was a sound on the road. I tensed, listening. It wasn't a car; it was nothing. Was I afraid of Doane returning and finding me here?

Of course I was afraid. I wasn't a fool.

Who said I wasn't a fool? There was more than a husband to fear.

Something like what Mr. Hickey had tried to tell me. One thing was sure: I wasn't happy about it. But there it was.

I tossed my cigarette away and got into my car. From in front of the barn the four dogs watched me malevolently.

Chapter Eight »»»

POLLY WELLMAN BROUGHT my mail out to me. She came around the grocery counter and handed it to me and whispered, "Harry, what did I do to make you mad at me?"

She needn't have whispered. It was the drowsy hour after lunch. She was tending both the store and the post office, and we were alone together for the first time since we had taken that walk to the creek.

I uttered a deprecating laugh. "What gives you that idea?"

"The way you've treated me since then. You come in here every day and act as if you hardly know me."

"What do you expect me to do with a store full of people and your parents around?"

"You might at least make a date. Or do you expect me to beg you?"

Footsteps approached from the back room of the store. Somebody chortled. "Is this the most private place you can pick?"

We were merely standing rather close together, but who-ever he was preferred to amuse himself by pretending he had embarrassed us. He was a nattily dressed man with a brush mustache under a button nose.

"You're an idiot, George," Polly said wearily and went back behind the counter.

He looked me over as he moved forward. "Say, don't I know you?"

I said I didn't think so. He frowned at me. Polly didn't bother to introduce us; angry with both of us, she busied herself straightening the candy display.

"I'll be damned!" he exclaimed. "You're Harry Wilde."

I admitted it.

"Sure," he said. "Guess you never saw me, but I've seen you play plenty of times. Me, I'm the prodigal son—George Wellman, Polly's big brother."

He stuck out a hand which I shook mechanically. He looked like any Eighth Avenue sharpie. What interested me about him was that he was the lad who a couple of years ago had brought Lela Doane to North Set. It was during this visit with him that night during which she had probably met Kenneth Doane for the first time.

"You know who he is, Polly?" he was saying. "The best damn playmaker in basketball. Without him the Gothams wouldn't be anywhere." He thumped my arm. "Say, what're you doing in this hick dump?"

I was wondering the same about him. Was he visiting his parents because Lela Doane lived in this village?

"I'm spending the summer here," I muttered.

"That so? Where?"

Mr. Hickey had said he was a gambler, and I had no use for the vermin who lived off my sweat. But there was no point in being impolite to Polly's brother in her presence. I told him I had rented the Hickey bungalow.

"Taking it easy, huh?" He nodded sympathetically. "Yeah, I heard you had a crackup. Over a dame, wasn't it?" He chortled. "It's always a dame."

From behind the counter Polly was listening wide-eyed. Her lower lip quivered.

"Well, I'll be going," I said. "Good-bye, Polly."

She tossed her head and said nothing. Again I hadn't asked her for a date.

"So long, Harry," George Wellman called. "Be seeing you around."

By the time I had walked halfway home, Polly was out of my thoughts. Another woman possessed them. I half expected to find that a note had been slipped under my door. There was nothing.

I read the newspaper. I did a tough double-crostic. I was grateful to that particularly fiendish form of puzzle because it kept my brain occupied. In the evening, Bill Hickey stopped in to suggest gin rummy. I got rid of him by saying I had a headache. I had to be alone in case Lela Doane showed up.

She didn't.

Next morning I passed up my pre-breakfast walk, remained in bed until ten. I wasn't tired; I just hadn't the will to do anything. I didn't go for the mail at all, and it was only partly because Polly would be there. That night I read until three in the morning.

I awoke to the sound of rain. For a long time I lay in bed listening to it. At noon I dressed and made lunch and started another double-crostic. But now even that was no good. I was beginning to appreciate the irony of Conrad Rickey's toast: To Maxine's suitors, our understanding and sympathy. I hadn't taken up an endless vigil outside Lela's door. But I was waiting.

The phone rang. Though she had said she would not risk a phone call, my heart leaped.

It was a woman's voice, but not the right one. Polly's voice.

"Harry, what are you doing on a rainy Sunday afternoon?"

Sunday? I had lost track. The last few days had become blurred.

"Sitting around," I said.

"It's a good afternoon for the movies."

I started to think up an excuse; then all of a sudden I knew I had to get away from the bungalow. This was my chance to escape complete demoralization.

"Sure thing," I said. "I'll pick you up as soon as I shave. Give me twenty minutes."

It was relaxing driving to Fort Able in the rain. Polly and I chattered about myself. She hadn't realized until her brother had told her that I was such a well-known athlete. I said shucks, there were a lot of better and more famous and certainly richer pros and there wasn't much future in it, and I entertained her with anecdotes about my teammates.

In the theater, she slipped her hand into mine. I held it cozily—a soft, warm, young hand. Not brown and strong and with a wedding ring on the third finger. I held her hand and after the picture we had a snack in a restaurant and she was sweet and pretty and it was pleasant being with her.

Until on the way home she said suddenly: "Harry, I love you."

She said it quietly; without turning her face to me.

I was terribly sorry. I groped for words, and those I finally uttered were no better than any others. "You don't mean it, Polly."

"I love you. I've no pride." She shifted along the seat and put her hand on my hand holding the wheel. "You must care for me or you wouldn't have made love to me like that at the creek."

"I was a heel, Polly."

She started to weep.

The rain pounded the car, washed the road, swayed the trees. I drove slowly into the downpour. Beside me she sniffled. I gave her my pocket handkerchief. She wiped her eyes and blew her nose.

"I—I can't help it," she quavered. "I wish I hated you, but I love you."

Almost I told her I wasn't worth it, but I caught myself in time, saving myself and her the meaningless cliché. I was silent.

"Harry, there's another woman, isn't there?"

"No." That was true and not true. I would have given her the same answer before I had ever met Lela Doane.

"There is," she insisted. "George said you'd cracked up over a woman. It was the woman who visited you last week, wasn't it?"

"We were divorced and that was that, I didn't crack up. I had too much basketball and needed a rest."

"Then what's wrong with me? You like me, don't you?"

"I'm very fond of you."

As I drove, I was thinking that I could be happy with her, happier than I had ever been with Gale, because it would be placid and well ordered. She would bring me the peace and emotional security I had lost when I had married Gale, and it wouldn't be hard to get to love her.

And Lela Doane? She was nobody who would ever be good for me.

A man didn't necessarily want what was good for him.

"Fond of me!" she said in quiet outrage. "And now, I guess, you wouldn't want to see me at all."

"Wouldn't that be better?"

"Please, Harry. Don't stay away. I couldn't stand it."

"All right," I said.

We had reached North Set. Night was descending early because of the storm. In the half-light, I glanced at her sitting huddled beside me. She raised her face, her round little jaw jutting defiantly.

"Harry, if there's another woman, I'll kill her before I'll let her have you."

I pulled up at the side of the store building.

"Stop talking nonsense," I said irritably.

"You think it's nonsense, do you?" She pushed open the door and ran across the rain to the entrance. I thought I heard her sob.

I wished, as I had never wished for anything, that this hadn't happened.

I was back in the bungalow for a full minute before I realized that I hadn't looked for a note from Lela Doane. I searched and didn't find one. The edge of disappointment had become slightly blunted. Maybe it was a good sign. More likely, I was only emotionally tired.

The storm had broken the heat spell; the weather was right for a fire. Days ago I had got in some exercise by borrowing from the Hickeys a band saw and wedges and sledge hammer and I had cut and split logs and filled the woodbin beside the fireplace. I built a fire and settled beside it with the Sunday Times I'd picked up in Fort Able.

I couldn't read. I gave up midway through the news and turned to the double-crostic in the magazine section. But I hadn't finished the one I had started that morning. I tried it again, and when I had the solution, I reread it several times:

"O. Henry: 'The Hiding of Black Bill.' 'A man asleep is certainly a sight to make angels weep. Now, a woman asleep you regard as different. No matter how she looks, you know it's better for all hands that she be that way.'

A wise man, O. Henry. I crumpled up the paper and tossed it into the fire. I put on two fresh logs and turned off all the lights and sat staring into the flames and listening to the rain on the roof. But only the setting was right for a man at peace. Everything else was wrong. If I'd had liquor in the house, it would have been a good time to get drunk.

I shouldn't have come to North Set. All I needed was some sense to pack up tomorrow and leave. There were other bungalows, other fire-places.

The door opened. She hadn't knocked. She just came in.

Chapter Nine »»»

RAIN SWIRLED IN with her. She closed the door quickly and stood against it to catch her breath. She looked utterly desirable in a belted navy-blue raincoat, and her wet and vivid face was framed by a plastic navy-blue kerchief over her hair and tied under her chin.

I was on my feet, but I didn't rush to her. We were strangers, constrained, though my heart pounded.

"Hello," I said, as if she were anybody at all dropping in for just a moment.

Lela Doane smiled, and I noticed how red and sensuously ripe her mouth was. It was the first make-up of any kind I had seen on her face.

She looked about. "A cozy place," she commented and moved leisurely into the room.

Little red boots like a child's reached up to the hem of her raincoat. She came toward me, but not to me. She paused at the table to put down her flashlight and went on to the fire where she stretched out her hands to its warmth.

I said, "Did you drive?"

"It would be dangerous to leave my car parked outside. Besides, I haven't got it."

"You walked all the way in the rain and the dark?"

"Major is with me."

"Is that the shepherd?"

"Yes. He's very devoted to me." She took off her kerchief. "Don't you think you ought to pull down the shades?"

And lock the door, I thought. I did that first. I pulled down the shades of the five living room windows and of the kitchen and bathroom windows—a deliberate and calculated act like everything else that had been said or done since her arrival, without any hint of the breathless and headlong passion that would be the only excuse for her being here.

Her kerchief was beside the flashlight on the table. Leisurely she was opening her raincoat. I came up behind her; she stirred only enough so that I could strip it down over her shoulders and arms. She stood ignoring me, staring into the flames—remote and straight-backed in a knitted green dress.

I hung the coat over the back of a wooden chair. When I turned back to her, she was lounging in the deep wing chair I had occupied when she had entered.

Lela extended her feet. "Take off my boots."

No please went with that request. And it wasn't a request; it was an order in a colorless, impersonal tone. I resented her attitude, resented her presence, resented the fact that I wanted her here and was kneeling at her feet as if in supplication.

I pulled the boots off. She wore brown-and-white low-heeled shoes and bobby socks. I removed the shoes and the socks. I held a bare foot in my hands, a smooth foot, unbroken and untwisted, with sleekly turned ankle and calf. I had an impulse to kiss it, but I didn't. Kneeling, holding her foot, I looked up at her.

Her face was turned sideways to the fire. Her profile was static, but not now empty; it seemed to be holding emotion in suspension, and there were purple shadows at the corners of her eyes.

I rose. I took out cigarettes and offered her one. She shook her head.

I said: "I suppose . . . he's out with the car?" I couldn't bring myself to say "your husband" or even his name.

"He's playing poker with friends. He'll be gone till one o'clock."

It was now twenty after nine. That gave us three hours and time for her to walk back. Plenty of time, even with this waiting. But waiting for what? Who was waiting for whom?

I tossed my cigarette into the fire and put my hands on the arms of the chair and bent over and kissed her. Her lips quivered under mine without parting, without ardent response. Suddenly she tore her mouth away and pushed me back from the chair and stood up.

I said querulously, "What'd you come here for then? Nobody forced you to."

When I stopped speaking, I could hear her breathe. Her face had changed. It had become sodden, and her eyes were heavy as if drugged.

"Undress me," she said hoarsely. "But slowly. Very slowly."

She remained standing in front of the fire. I found the zipper at the side of her knitted dress. She didn't help me at all. Slowly, she had said—an order, a ritual, like taking off her boots. The little she had on under the dress was simpler, but I made this slower still, lingering, caressing. Then I stepped back and looked at her in the gentle and mellow glow of the flames.

Conrad Hickey was right, her figure was fuller than I had thought. But not the way he had painted it, not fleshy. Ripe and at the same time firm, deep only where a mature woman should be, and her skin was like tan satin.

Lela was smiling now, warmly, liking me to look at her. She lifted my hands and placed them on her hips and her own hands pulled my face down to hers and her body arched taut as a bowstring against mine. The play was all hers. I was tagging along with her, obeying the moods of her desire. That was all right because our desires coincided.

Her hands, still holding my face, curved; the sharp fingernails dug into my cheeks.

"Hey, that hurts!"

She laughed, or maybe not a laugh so much as an expulsion of breath. She ran across the room and threw herself face down on the bed and waited for me.

Moments later, I wondered how I could have thought her remote and restrained and withdrawn.

I must have dozed off. I awoke gradually, remembering. Drowsily, I felt beside me. I was alone in bed, and, with a sense of great loss, I thought it must have been a dream. Against my eyeballs brightness glared. I opened my eyes and there she was sitting at the fire.

She sat on her legs. She must have built up the fire, for it was blazing, sending dancing highlights of shadow over her naked body. Her back was to me. She had taken down her hair; it hung gleaming black in firelight to her shoulders.

She was beautiful. I knew that now.

"Like me any better?" I said.

She looked at me over a bare shoulder. For the first time she really smiled, full-mouthed, generously. I had learned that after all she was capable of more emotion-physical emotion, anyway—than any woman I had known.

"A little," she said. "Come here to the fire. Bring the blanket."

I gathered up the blanket crumpled at the foot of the bed. She rose to help me spread it out in front of the fire and we lay down side by side. Our heels touched the edge of the hearth, and, as we lay on the blanket listening to the rain and the wind, the heat of the fire spread up along our bodies. I had found peace.

She turned her head on my shoulder and said: "I'd like to see you play basketball. You must be very graceful."

"I suppose George Wellman told you I'm a basketball player."

"George? Do you know him?"

"He's in North Set."

"Is he?" she said indifferently.

Her voice had become flat again. Her cheek was on my shoulder; so I couldn't see her face—not that I could have told from looking at her whether she was lying. But why should I care? I had as much of her as I ought to want.

It wasn't that simple.

"How did you find out about me?" I persisted.

"Perhaps because I'm interested in you."

She had told me as much as she wanted to, and that was little.

I said: "All right, I'm interested in you. Tell me about yourself;"

"There's nothing."

"You come from New York, don't you?"

"From Pennsylvania, but I lived in New York for a while."

"Alone?"

She stirred a little. "Yes. I was a salesgirl in a department store."

"Was that where you married Kenneth Doane—in New York?"

She let a silence pass before she said, "Yes," and after that there was no more talk.

You couldn't get anywhere near her with words. With her they weren't a means of communication. It occurred to me that even at the height of our love-making she hadn't uttered the usual terms of endearment—the almost automatic expressions of love or affection or pleasure that, the intensity of such moments calls forth. Only the little gasps, the rhythmic moans that had had no unique and special significance outside the act itself.

Why should I have wanted more than that from her? Lying here snug on a blanket with her in the warm glow of the fire was complete in itself. It was enough. I felt that it was the best we could give each other.

I lifted my head to look at the clock on the dresser.

"What time is it?" she muttered.

"Close to eleven."

"There's time."

This was the bad part—that we should fear time.

"Suppose he comes home earlier and finds you out?" I said.

"He's never home from a poker game before one."

"But suppose this time he does?"

She didn't bother to answer.

I turned on my side, looking at her. She lay utterly still with her eyes closed. She was beautiful by firelight. I kissed her and she reached for me.

"Yes," she said. "Yes, yes."

It was twenty after twelve when I again looked at the clock.

I heard the shower going in the bathroom. The door was open, but from where I lay on the blanket I couldn't see her. The fire had sunk to glowing ashes.

I roused myself and renewed the fire with kindling and a few small logs. I went to the closet and put on my robe and slippers. On the way back I glanced into the bathroom. The shower curtain was drawn around the tub. I lit a cigarette and settled myself in the wing chair.

Lela came out drying herself with a bath towel. She had pinned up her hair and somehow had kept it from getting wet. Without glancing at me, she moved to the hearth. I watched the languorous sway of her hips. She crouched at the fire, letting the heat finish drying her. The moistness of her satiny skin in that radiance gave it a golden sheen.

"Let me have a cigarette," she said.

"I thought you didn't smoke."

"Sometimes I do."

I lit one and handed it to her. I twisted my head to the clock.

"It's almost twelve-thirty," I told her. "You'd better hurry."

She said tauntingly into the fire, "You're afraid of him."

"I'm afraid for you."

"He wouldn't hurt me."

"He'd hurt only me—is that it?"

"I don't know."

Anger touched me—anger at her, at him, at being afraid. "Are you sure he wouldn't hurt you? Are you sure he wouldn't do to you what he did to—"

I stopped. It was a foolish thing to say. I had stopped for another reason too. She had leaped to her feet. She was facing me, trembling, and now there was too much expression in her contorted face.

"Don't say that!" she cried. "Don't ever say that again!"

"Take it easy, Lela. There's no need—"

"You've no right to say it, do you hear?"

Her words were like a low scream. She stood hugging herself, trembling, and I saw that she was ridden by terror.

"My God," I said, "you're scared sick of him!"

"No. That's a lie."

"Why go back to him? Why stay with him?"

"Don't! You don't know what you're saying."

She went to her clothes, started to dress with fumbling fingers, her breasts heaving. Momentarily her head disappeared as she pulled the green knitted dress down over it, and when I saw her face again it was as if a whisked curtain had changed the scene and character. Abruptly, she was completely calm, drawn back into herself—the transformation as startling as her outburst.

She smiled. "I guess I was pretty silly. But those stories annoy me."

"Is that all it was?"

"Of course." She sat down to put on her socks and shoes and boots.

"Lela, let me help you," I said.

"You mean dress?"

"You know what I mean."

She rose and I held her raincoat for her. She tied her rain kerchief, picked up her flashlight. She hadn't answered me; she had, as usual, simply stopped talking. There were no more words, not even good-bye. A kiss after I had unlocked the door, a brief brushing of lips, and she was gone.

I closed the door and pulled up a window shade. Her flashlight cut through the night. In its splash I saw that the rain had turned to drizzle, and I saw the big German shepherd rise from the side of the bungalow and silently accompany her.

Chapter Ten »»»

MONDAY AFTERNOON the battered station wagon rolled up my driveway. I heard the squeak and rattle of it, and when I reached the front window it had stopped behind my coupe and Kenneth Doane was getting out.

I wondered how he had found out about the night before and what he proposed to do about it.

Knuckles rapped on the door. My eyes fell on the fire poker. It would be a weapon of some sort. He knocked again.

I wiped my mouth with the back of my hand and, without the poker, I went to the door and pulled it open.

Doane didn't look at all unfriendly. He gave me a piece of a smile. "Hello. I picked up something for you at the Fort Able express office."

"For me?" I said.

"I was in the express office and they asked me if I knew a Harry Wilde in North Set. They had three packages for you; so I took them along."

I felt pretty silly.

"That was swell of you," I said.

"Well, I was passing here anyway."

I went with him to the station wagon. He unfastened the rear door and handed out to me two packages. They were from Dave Morrison. The third package was flat and so large that it just about fitted into the station wagon at an angle. Together we tugged it out and eased it down to the ground.

"It looks like a basketball backboard," I said.

Doane nodded. "I played a bit in college, but football was my game. I hear you're one of the great ones. What's your team?"

"The New York Gothams."

"I follow sports, though mostly football and baseball. Weren't you the champs last year?"

"We finished second in the league and lost the final play-off."

"That so?" he said vaguely, not really interested. He ran a hand through his wiry blond hair.

"How about a beer?" I suggested.

"No, thanks, I've got to get back." He climbed into his station wagon and started the wheezing engine.

"By the way, Doc," I said, "how's my dog?"

"Fine. Just fine."

He drove off.

For a minute we had become practically chummy, and he had done me a favor. I was sorry he had. I wanted to owe him nothing, and I would have preferred to dislike him thoroughly.

I carried the two smaller packages into the bungalow and opened them. I'd guessed correctly. One contained a molded rubber basketball, already inflated, and the other a hoop and net and brackets. That left no doubt that the flat package outside was a backboard.

Dave Morrison hadn't written me that he was sending them,

but they spoke for themselves. The coach thought I'd had enough of loafing; the least I could do from here on was to keep my shooting eye sharpened. It was a fine idea. I'd never got the habit of doing absolutely nothing, of being utterly useless, and, for me, basketball wasn't a sport but a profession.

Halfway up my driveway, there was a pole that fed both the Hickey house and the bungalow with electric and telephone wires. It was high enough for the backboard, and there was plenty of room in front and at the sides, but the ground was pretty rough. I borrowed tools from the Hickeys and raked and leveled and pounded that area.

I worked until dark and all next day. By late afternoon, I was ready to put up the backboard, but it was too heavy for me to handle alone. When Bill Hickey came home, I asked him to give me a hand. He fetched a ladder and rope, and in the twilight we raised the backboard and fastened it to the pole while Mr. Hickey acted as foreman and Mrs. Hickey as audience.

At ten o'clock Tuesday night, I flopped into bed dead tired. It wasn't like after a hard game, when exhaustion was in my belly and nerves. This was a vigorous, healthy weariness of muscles having done unaccustomed work. I felt fine. I slept like a rock with hardly a thought about Lela Doane.

Wednesday morning I started pouring the ball through the basket. Conrad Hickey came out of the house and watched me.

"Don't you ever miss?" he asked.

"Too often, in a game. It's a lot simpler here where a couple of giants aren't mobbing you and you have to get the ball away in a split second off your right ear. Besides, my job isn't primarily to score. Only when convenient."

I hit a one-handed push from forty feet out. I drove in and floated the ball through like a balloon. I was feeling better and better.

Mr. Hickey said abruptly: "One thing that's been puzzling me about Alice Doane is that after she left North Set with her husband she never communicated with the School Board."

I missed an easy hook shot. I retrieved the ball and looked at him. His pinched face was blandly innocent.

"You told me you don't approve of gossip," I said.

"As a lawyer, I approve of evidence. I doubt that Doane could afford to send her alimony, and she had no family to support her. She'd naturally go back to teaching—if not in North Set, elsewhere. But she couldn't teach anywhere without sending back here for her record."

"Maybe after her divorce she married a man who could support her adequately. Or became interested in another kind of job. I can think up a dozen reasons."

"So can I, but let me finish. Did I tell you I used to be on the School Board? I was defeated in the last election because I believe schools should educate children, and of course taxpayers wouldn't stand for that. Costs too much. Well, before Alice went away that summer, she signed a contract to teach the third grade the following year. She knew the school was depending on her. When school opened in September, no Alice. We waited a whole week, and then it was another month before we could find a teacher to replace her. Alice was a considerate girl; she wouldn't have done that to the children and to the school. It wouldn't have taken her two minutes to write or wire that she wouldn't be back."

I threw the ball in a line drive. It hit the front of the rim and bounded toward the road.

"Not a word," Mr. Hickey mused. "I can't believe that of Alice."

I brought the ball back slowly. "Why the hell don't you tell that to your son? He's a cop."

"Bill's stubborn. He says it's not a cop's business if a girl wants to divorce her husband and not teach school any more."

"What makes it my business?"

"As I recall, Harry, you were curious about the Doanes. I'm simply making conversation."

Simply! The way last week he had simply shown me that painting of Lela as he had imagined her nude and had uttered words of warning against her which I had felt he had intended to have exactly the opposite effect. Was he up to something now, and if so what and why?

I dribbled the ball to the basket for a floating lay-up and turned to ask him, but he had wandered off into the house. I was sure he wouldn't have told me anyway.

I marked off a foul line and dumped them in from there.

George Wellman came sauntering up the road. He was quite a sight in cream-colored slacks and a sport shirt decorated with spirals in half a dozen garish colors. Because North Set wasn't a resort town, nobody else dressed like that.

"I brought your mail," he announced. "Polly says you haven't picked it up since Saturday."

I'd been too busy with manual labor the last couple of days to go to the post office. But that was the superficial reason—the excuse. After what Polly had said to me in my car in the rain late Sunday afternoon and after what had happened in my bungalow that night, I hadn't been anxious to face her. Where women are concerned, especially women who say they love you when you don't want them to, a man can be a gosh-awful coward.

"Thanks," I said and took the letters and newspapers from him and put them on a rock.

"Tuning up for the coming season, huh?" George observed amiably.

I grunted and picked up the ball and shot from all angles. I doubted that he had taken a walk in the heat to bring me my mail. He took his time getting around to whatever it was.

I said: "What do you find to keep you around North Set?"

"Easiest place to get bored to death, isn't it?" he said. "Staying with the folks is a cheap way to get away from the sidewalks of New York, which aren't fit for humans in summer. Happens I'm broke." He fingered his brush mus-tache. "Expect a good year with the Gothams?"

"Why not?"

"Yeah. You'll have one or two more good years, then you'll slow up. You're no kid any more. Then what'll you do?"

"Coach, or teach, or mooch quarters."

"How'd you like to make real dough while you still can?"

I hefted the ball in my right hand as if to throw it into his face. But I wasn't going to. He didn't bother me that much. I said without heat: "Beat it."

"Don't get sore, pal. I didn't say you should throw games."

"That's damn generous of you."

"The Gothams can win and you can pick up heavy dough at the same time. It's a snap in basketball on account of the betting's on a point spread. Say there's a game where your team's a seven-point favorite on the books. You come down to the final minutes leading by say, ten points. Now you're the playmaker; you're the guy the team works around. So your passing suddenly isn't so sharp; you lose a ball a couple times; you're off on your shooting and you can't find the basket on fouls. Nobody sees anything fishy; a guy gets tired and even Harry Wilde makes mistakes. The Gothams still win, but you make sure by less than seven points, and we collect. Get the idea?"

I said: "I get the idea that I can have you jailed for attempted bribery."

He leered. "You wouldn't do that to Polly's brother, now would you? Besides, where's a witness?"

"Beat it," I said.

George watched the ball in my hand as if it were a bomb. His tongue flicked over his lips, but he didn't give up.

"Don't be a sap, pal. Who loses? The Gothams don't. It's a won game in the standings if they win by one point or twenty. The bookies get hurt, that's all. You're not worried about the bookies, are you?"

"I'm worried about you," I said. "In about ten seconds I'm going to ram this ball down your throat."

I hefted the ball.

George Wellman left. He didn't quite run, but he moved rapidly and kept glancing over his shoulder.

That bumbling heel was the lad who had brought Lela up to North Set, and whatever she had been or hadn't been to him at that time, she must have run around with the gambler crowd of which he was a part. Had she been as quiet and indrawn then, before she had buried herself away in this small village as the wife of the local veterinary? What matter? I didn't know anything about her except that she made love wonderfully without its being love.

I picked up the basketball, but I had lost interest. North Set had turned out to be no place for taking life easy, for having nothing on my mind. It wasn't even a place where you could shoot baskets without being vastly disturbed by a neighbor who kept pricking your mind and nerves with dark hints and speculations and who thought he had reason to believe he could induce you to sell yourself.

I went inside and read my mail and showered and shaved and ate an early lunch. Then, in the midday heat, I went out for a walk.

For several days I had not walked anywhere. I headed north through woods and fields to the clearing where two weeks ago Maxine had dumped two bones at my feet.

Beside the clearing and behind the spread of sumac, a knoll rose rather steeply. It was so rocky that little vegetation could grow on it. I climbed to the top and had quite a view of an uninhabited valley on my right and a piece of the village on my left. Directly ahead, beyond a couple of boulder-strewn meadows, stood the Doane barn and house.

I had half expected that because the direction was about right, but I hadn't thought that the Doanes would live quite so close. In my two previous visits I had approached this area at an angle through woods. No other building was anywhere near.

I descended the knoll, mostly by sliding on my heels. There was too much rock for the digging of a fairly deep hole that would have to be six feet long. I skirted around the sumac and climbed a stone wall to the first of the two meadows. This was too open and, anyway, farther than where Maxine must have found the bones.

I was staring at the knoll when I heard the dogs. I spun around to see all four of them tearing at me from the Doane place.

"Down!" I said as they came up to me.

The familiar command may have influenced them; more likely they recognized me from my two previous visits as not quite a stranger. Three of them, though they continued their vicious uproar, kept their distance. Major, the big shepherd who had accompanied Lela to my bungalow Sunday night, became positively amiable, accepting me as a friend because his mistress had done the same. He sniffed at my feet and wagged his tail happily when I patted his head.

It was too late to slip away. Somebody from the house might have seen me. Anyway, why not go on? Dr. Doane had done me a favor Monday and he was boarding my dog. What was more natural than to stop by for a drink of water while out for a walk? Only my conscience would be able to find anything wrong in that.

Escorted by the dogs, I walked on. I saw two cars between the barn and the house—the station wagon and a red sedan. Evidently the Doanes had visitors.

"Hello?" I heard Doane call out when I reached the back of the barn. "Who's there?"

I rounded the corner of the barn. The visitor was Gale.

Chapter Eleven »»»

GALE HELD MAXINE cradled in her arms. Doane stood beside her, and I can't say I'd ever seen a handsomer couple—if they could be considered a couple.

"Why, Hair-y, of all people!" she said brightly.

Doane nodded vaguely and shuffled his feet and stuck his hands out of the way into his pants pockets. He had the poise of a nine-year-old boy.

I said: "I live here in North Set—remember?"

"I drove up to visit Max." Gale stuck her lovely chin at the red sedan. "I borrowed that car from Augie Random. You remember Augie Random, darling."

I made no effort to remember Augie Random. It was doubtful that during our brief marriage I had met all the men from whom she could borrow cars. I fished out a cigarette and lit it.

A lot of rumbling went on about us. It was from the four dogs, particularly the two males who were looking up longingly at Maxine without daring to make much of a fuss because of the presence of Doane. Maxine stirred restlessly against Gale's splendid bosom.

"I think we'd better take her back," Doane suggested. "Let me have her."

"Oh, no, I'll carry him," Gale said—him still meaning Maxine. "I've missed him so."

Passionately she pushed her face into Maxine's fur as Doane opened the gate. Side by side, they walked across the paddock, leaving me there alone.

I waited. From where I stood, I wasn't far from the corner kitchen window, and through it I saw movement. Lela could see me more easily; she must have known that I was outside, but she didn't come to the window to say hello.

I lit a second cigarette from the stub of my first. They were returning. Gale looked citified and out of place in an immense straw picture hat and a tight yellow silk dress. Her head was tilted sideways and up to Doane and she was smiling readily and speaking animatedly. He didn't answer; he walked beside her and held himself awkwardly stiff. They should get along well, I thought; she was good at carrying on one-sided conversations.

When they were through the paddock gate, Doane veered off to the house. Gale brought her set and meaningless smile over to me.

"Darling, let me have a cigarette," she said. "I ran out of mine, and Dr. Doane doesn't smoke."

I had never known her when she hadn't run out of cigarettes. I held a match for her and said: "Did you stop off at my bungalow?"

"I thought I would on the way back, but now I won't have time because Mrs. Doane invited me for lunch. Anyway, I'm seeing you now, aren't I?"

"For lunch?" I said. "Mrs. Doane invited you?"

"What's so surprising about being invited for lunch?"

"Nothing, I suppose. How're you doing with Doane?"

"Doing?"

"Are you making any progress with him?"

Gale brushed tobacco off her lower lip. "What in the world are you talking about?"

"You know what I'm talking about," I said. "This isn't the first time you've seen him since you met him at the swimming pool."

"Hair-y, how can you imagine such a thing? I drove here to visit Max."

"How did you know where she was?"

"How? Why . . ." She paused to think up a good one and flubbed it. "Why, you told me on the phone you'd taken Max to the kennels."

"I told you I was going to. At the time, I didn't know where I was going to take her. If you'd come up here to see Maxine, you would've stopped at my bungalow to find out where she was. You didn't have to because you'd already talked to Doane."

"Hair-y, even if it were true—it's not, but if it were— I'm no longer your wife."

Gale had me there. And after Sunday night, who was I to cast the first stone?

"And when we were married," she went on petulantly, "did I ever cheat on you?"

"Probably not, though when I was on the road with the team I used to wonder about all those men you knew."

"So it's a crime for a girl to have friends."

"You're changing the subject. I'm talking about the present, about you and this small-town Nature Boy."

"You've no right to make such nasty-minded insinuations."

No right, perhaps, but I didn't like these circles spreading within circles. Things were becoming too complicated for a guy who was here for a summer of restful and unemotional living.

"I just want to get the record straight," I muttered.

"All right, Hair-y. The record is that I'm delighted to be rid of you and I'll stop people calling me Mrs. Wilde."

"Check, Miss Holmstrom," I said. That was her maiden name.

She brought out the child in me. This kind of infantile squabbling was one of the things that had wrecked our marriage.

We stood smoking in silence. There was nothing to keep me there, not this woman nor the one in the house either, but I stayed, and suddenly she smiled.

"Let's remain good friends, shall we, darling?" she said.

You couldn't stay mad at Gale. She never let a quarrel stretch out for more than a few minutes, not even with an ex-husband.

"Sure," I said.

Lela Doane came out on the porch in her gingham dress.

All I got from her was a vague nod. She could hardly have thrown her arms around my neck, but she could have spared more than that with propriety.

"Lunch is ready, Mrs. Wilde," she said.

Gale stepped on her cigarette. "Good-bye, darling." She kissed my chin to demonstrate a renewal of friendliness then walked rather gingerly over the uneven ground on heels that were too high. Her lithe hips swayed invitingly.

Lela waited for her on the porch. For a moment they stood together, and by contrast Lela may have looked drab and almost unattractive, but I wouldn't know because my reaction to her was now tied up with the memory of her in my bungalow by firelight.

I walked home by way of the road.

At six o'clock, I was peeling potatoes to go with a steak when the phone rang. I didn't at once recognize the voice that said impassively: "Mr. Wilde?"

"Yes. Who's this?"

"Mrs. Doane."

That voice, without a face and body to go with it, was utterly without personality. But why was she phoning? She herself had pointed out the risk of being overheard on a party wire.

"Yes?" I said cautiously.

"Mrs. Wilde left a message. You know that she was here to see her dog."

"I know."

"She asked me to tell you that she decided to drive back to New York."

It didn't make sense. Gale had made it clear that she wouldn't stop off at the bungalow. Anyway, she herself could have called from the Doane house.

"Is she still there?" I asked.

"No. They left an hour ago. My husband has some business in New York. He had intended to go by train this afternoon, but he decided to leave a little later and save fare by taking a lift with her."

So I had made nasty-minded insinuations! But that was all right with me. In fact, it was fine because what Lela had phoned to tell me was that she would be alone all night. They wouldn't reach New York until nine or ten, and if conceivably he wanted to return immediately, there would be no train until next morning.

"I see," I said.

"Thanks for that book you loaned me," she said. "I'm going to read it tonight."

That meant that this time she wanted me to come to her.

"I'm sure you'll find it an exciting book, Mrs. Doane. Good-bye."

"Good-bye, Mr. Wilde."

I hung up. I looked at my wrist watch. Twelve minutes after six. It wouldn't be completely dark until nine—say a quarter after nine to play safe. Three hours.

Chapter Twelve »»»

THE HOUSE WAS DARK and the dogs were quiet. I had walked all the way because my car must not be observed parked at her house. I stood on the road and listened to the silence.

Had I misinterpreted her message? Had she also gone for the night or was she at this moment on the way to my bungalow? Then what had been the meaning of her statement that she was staying home with a nonexistent book?

I doused my flashlight. The new moon was still too low to help; I groped my way across the bare area and almost walked into the station wagon. Something rubbed against my leg. I knew it was Major because he was silent and friendly. She must have locked the other dogs in the barn, leaving the shepherd out as a watch dog. She wouldn't have gone anywhere except to my bungalow without driving, and Major would have escorted her if she had walked in the night.

I whispered, "Hi, Major," and wondered why I whispered. His tail wagged against my leg. He was kinder than I. Almost two weeks ago I hadn't let him get near Maxine, but being a dog and not human he treated me a lot better now when I was coming to his house for the same basic purpose. Maybe that wasn't a nice way to put it, but a dog couldn't appreciate the distinction.

The sagging porch steps creaked under my feet. The small sound was startling in the night. Distantly a dog—no doubt Maxine—started to bark stridently, and the dogs in the barn took it up. But not for long; by the time I entered the house the silence was back, outside and inside.

The only light in the living room flowed dimly down from the head of the staircase. It touched in vague outline the painting of her above the fireplace. I waited amid the mohair furniture. She must have heard the dogs and the slam of the screen door and must know I was in the house, there was no sign of her presence, no sound from her.

The kitchen was dark. I moved over the threadbare rug and shone my flashlight down a short hall.

"Lela," I called softly.

No answer.

There was a sense of terror here. Maybe, I thought, because a dark and empty house that should be neither dark nor empty created its own doubt and uneasiness, or maybe because my imagination was working on stories heard and bones Maxine had found very near here. I laughed a little, but it was silent laughter centered in the pit of my stomach.

There was, after all, a dim light at the head of the stairs. A beacon perhaps. I went up the stairs. These creaked, too. Rather, they groaned under my feet as if in weary protest at being violated, as I was violating this household. I wasn't much good at this sort of thing. I was plagued with a conscience.

I paused. She must have heard that creaking if she was in the house. But she did not come forward or call out, and I went on.

In the square hall upstairs, I was confronted by four closed doors. I opened the nearest and looked into a rather large bedroom. I played the flashlight beam on a double bed, on a plain wooden chair. Then I closed the door, glad at any rate that she was not awaiting me in that room, which, no doubt, was the one she shared with her husband.

"Lela!" I called angrily.

The silence was digging in under my skin, seeming to quiver against raw flesh. I kicked open a door and found a bathroom with ancient, discolored fixtures. I swung to the far end of the hall and pushed that door in, and light greeted me.

Not much light. It came from a table lamp scarcely brighter than a candle, and it reached out as diffused and gentle as starlight to envelope her where she stood facing me at a window with the night behind her.

I stepped in and closed the door. This was also a bedroom, but smaller than the other. The bed looked narrower, and the only other furniture it contained was a chest of drawers on which the lamp stood and a chair against the wall. The spare bedroom, the guest room and I was a guest who sneaked in at night and whom she was receiving in a pale nightgown.

Her only response to my entrance was to smile as a shadow might smile, and I said hello. It was like a casual greeting in the street between two people who didn't know each other well—except that there was the bed with the cover turned down and her half-exposed breasts swelling up above the negligible bodice of the nightgown, which was made of some transparent stuff through which her body shimmered ripely.

She must have been standing there for quite some time, watching from the window for my flashlight on the road and then listening to me fumble my way closer and closer to her, perhaps savoring the anticipation, even now holding herself withdrawn, making a peculiar game of it which she had played with me from the first, a game of holding back until everything pent up in both of us had to explode.

I closed the door, but I did not go to her. It was a game two could play. Grinning, I said: "What would you have done if I'd decided you weren't home and had left without coming up here?"

"If you want me enough, you'll always find me."

"So it's not so much a teasing game as a ritual. Well, that's all right with me."

Lela's hands moved slowly around the rich curves of her hips and down and lay spread on her thighs. The nightgown was nylon, a pink mist over her tan body swelling into it.

"You're here now," she said with an intensity I'd never before heard in her voice. "You're here, and do you have to keep talking?"

I had a notion to make her come to me, to make her fling herself at me. But there was no point to it; I didn't feel vindictive. Two strides took me to her. The nylon slid under my hands; it exuded the luscious warmth of her flesh. I slid down the shoulder straps and pressed her breasts into my face. Her fingers drove into the nape of my neck. She pushed my mouth up to hers, and, in the hungry kiss, she twisted herself and me with her around to the bed and fell back on it without releasing me.

Somewhere around midnight, I stood at the window buttoning my shirt.

The dim table lamp was still on; it had not been off at any

time. On the bed she slept. A breeze touched with coolness had swirled in a while ago and she had pulled up the blanket, but it lay only as far as her hips. Absently I wondered what had happened to the pink nightgown; I could not recall at just what moment it had completely disappeared.

I lit a cigarette and tossed the match out through the window. The new moon had risen high enough to outline the squatting barn and beyond it, against the darker sky of stars, the knoll from which that afternoon I had looked in this direction.

"Are you afraid of him?" she said.

She had awakened or perhaps she had not really been asleep. Her arm remained limply on the pillow where I had shifted it from across my chest when I had left the bed. Her mouth and jaw were slack with sleep or something else, but there was no sleep in her dark eyes that caught sultry glints of light like sparks from the lamp.

"Afraid?" I echoed, though I knew very well what she meant.

"He won't be back till tomorrow afternoon." Scorn tinged her voice. "You can stop worrying."

"You're the one who's worrying. What makes you so scared of him?"

"Me?"

"Any psychologist will tell you that you talk so much about me being afraid of him because you're the one who is."

She started to yawn and pushed her face into the pillow to stifle it. She spoke against the pillow. "You dressed though there's no need to leave yet. Then you say I'm afraid."

"I've been here three hours," I argued. "I figured that was enough for one night."

She kicked the blanket off and stretched sensuously. Maybe

that wasn't a deliberate attempt to express what no words could say anywhere nearly as convincingly, but it did the trick. She was at her best like this, in firelight or with the glow of a very dim bulb enveloping her in caressing high-lighted shadows. I wanted to bury my face in her flesh and tell her that I loved her. With any other woman at such a time it would have been the natural thing to do, but some-how not with her.

I knew that I would stay, and so there was no hurry. I flicked ashes out of the window and brooded upon the humped knoll across two meadows.

"How far does your property extend?" I asked.

"Why?"

I couldn't bring myself to tell her about the bones Maxine had found there. I said: "I took a walk this afternoon and saw this house from that knoll back there. That's how I happened to come blundering this way. Does the knoll be-long to you?"

"This property belongs to Kenneth."

"Including that knoll?"

"I really don't know. There are about twenty acres, I understand, but I've little idea what they include." She paused. "Why? Are you thinking of buying him out, with me thrown in?"

That was the first attempt at humor I had heard her make, and she said it with a husky little laugh, but I thought I detected acid in her tone.

"I'd like to get you away from him," I told her quietly, "in any way I can."

Perhaps that was more than I had meant to say, but I couldn't be coldly reasonable, standing there by the window and looking down at her, uncovered and desirable beyond thought.

"No," she said and turned her face on the pillow.

Nothing more than that. No discussion; no statement about how she felt about me. Impulsively I had thrown myself at her feet, and all I got in return was the briefest possible negative, followed by the usual silence.

"Why don't you ever want to talk?" I said testily.

"About what?"

"About any subject that comes close to you. Let's start with a simple one. Where do we go from here?"

Her hand moved languidly in her mass of loose black hair. "Why should we go anywhere?"

"Well, we can't go on like this."

She didn't ask why we couldn't or argue about it or discuss it. This was another subject she simply dropped. With her cheek on the pillow, she watched me.

"Come back to bed," she said huskily.

So that was the beginning and the end of it; come back to bed. It wasn't enough. But what did I really want?

As I continued to stand there, despising her and myself, she flung her legs to the side of the bed and raised her shoulders as if to get out. Then she sank back and lay completely limp, her mouth slack and her eyes half-closed.

"Come to bed," she whispered.

I sat on the bed and untied my shoes. She was reaching for me before I could get them off.

And this was the only thing we had between us, that we shared completely, giving and taking. But only up to a point, only physically. Once sheer emotion broke past my throat and I held her fiercely, gasping, "I love you, Lela, I love you," and, though her body and hands and mouth remained possessive, she gave no vocal response, uttered no words to match my own, not even the lies or automatic phrases of romance that are expected at such a time, nothing but the searing ardor of the flesh and a sense that, though I had all of her, I had none of her.

The night was long and eventually I slept and in the morning I awoke with the sun in my eyes.

She was not in the room. My wrist watch told me that it was after nine. I lay in the splash of sunlight and listened to water run downstairs. Suddenly I hated being there. I dressed quickly.

Lela was frying bacon in the kitchen. Evidently the only thing she had on beside slippers was what my mother used to call a wrapper. I hadn't seen any woman wear one in years. It was calico and pretty scant, sleeveless and didn't quite reach her knees, and it was faded and slightly soiled. But, somehow, on her it didn't look bad. It made her appear rather girlish, the way it fitted so snugly and exposed her trim legs and brown arms and tended to fall away from her bosom, and I liked the way her black hair hung loosely to her shoulders.

She raised her head and said gaily: "Good morning. Breakfast is practically ready."

I lifted her chin with a finger and looked into her dark eyes. "Let's hear you say good morning with my name after it."

"Why?"

"I don't expect you to say that you care for me or even like me or that you'll call me darling or sweetheart. But you've never said my name and I wonder how it sounds on your lips."

"Good morning, Harry," she said with a smile that was very full for her.

I kissed her and went to the table already set for two, and we started to eat breakfast.

For a few minutes I had felt as if I were coming down to the first morning of a honeymoon. But that was a fraud. This was another man's house, her husband's house, and soon he would return and tonight he would be with her in that bed in that other bedroom I had glanced into last night.

Over the ham and eggs, I made a frontal attack. "How do you feel about your husband spending the night in New York with Gale?"

"Gale?" she said frowning.

"The woman he drove with to New York, who, incidentally, happens to be my ex-wife. It's becoming quite involved, isn't it?"

"He took the ride with her because he had to go to New York anyway on business."

"You believe that?"

Lela was not at all disturbed. "You don't understand Kenneth."

"I realize that, but I'm trying to. Of course we mustn't expect their morals to be better than ours."

"That's absurd." A corner of her mouth twitched. "He told me several days ago that he was going to New York. Anyway, he wouldn't look at another woman."

"I see," I said. "You prefer to believe that you can eat your cake and have it."

She tossed her loose hair and picked up her coffee pot and poured. "I never knew anybody who jabbered as much as you."

"That's right, I talk," I told her bitterly. "I try to complicate things. If I had your sense, I'd take my pleasure and be satisfied."

"Well, why not?" she said.

In the barn, the dogs set up a clamor.

Lela stiffened, listening. "Somebody is coming," she whispered and stood up. She paused with a hand on the back of the chair; her face was drawn into tense angles. She said, "Don't let anybody see you here," and left the kitchen, hurrying across the living room to intercept whoever it was at the front door. One of the dogs was barking directly under the kitchen window. That would be Major, who hadn't been locked in the barn overnight. Abruptly I stood up. Major would be sticking close to the visitor, and Major was near the back door.

Before I was halfway across the kitchen, a face appeared in the back door window—a face that smirked knowingly at me.

Chapter Thirteen »»»

GEORGE WELLMAN STEPPED into the kitchen. He grinned at the table set for two.

"Well, well, what d'you know? I come to visit Lela for old time's sake and find she has company for breakfast. She always liked 'em tall like you, Harry." He leered past me. "Don't you, Lela?"

She had returned to the kitchen. She stood just inside the doorway and said in that tone that indicated no interest or concern or anything: "Mr. Wilde stopped in to see his dog that we're boarding for him. I invited him to have coffee."

"Now isn't that nice?" he purred. "That's more than you ever did for me, baby, and I've known you lots longer. That's quite an outfit you're wearing for receiving strange company."

She drew her skimpy cotton wrapper tighter about herself.

It was time for me to say a piece. "I usually take an early morning walk," I explained. "I happened to be near here."

"I bet you happened." George nodded happily. "I bet you happen to be near here mostly at night when her husband isn't home."

I didn't let my fist push that smirk through his face because I couldn't afford to.

Holding the wrapper pulled across her breasts, Lela moved past me to the table. Like myself, she ignored his remark. "Would you like to have coffee with us, George?"

"I had breakfast a while ago. All I want to do is tell you a little story."

He sat down at the table and crossed his legs and fingered his mustache like the villain in an old-time melodrama. Lela and I remained standing.

"This story starts late yesterday afternoon," he said. "I'm in my old man's store when Doc Doane comes in to buy a pack of cigarettes. Polly waits on him. She says she thought he didn't smoke and he says they're for a lady he got a ride with to New York. I'm standing by the window and see him get in a car with a snappy blonde behind the wheel. Polly sees her too and tells me she's your divorced wife, Harry. So, okay; it don't figure yet. At night I have nothing to do, so I take a walk to your bungalow to talk some basketball. You're not home, but your car's outside. Now that's funny. You can't go anywhere here without a car unless to a close neighbor."

The car, I thought. It was almost as much of a mistake to have left it outside my bungalow when I was gone for the night as it would have been to park it here. I was quite inexperienced in this kind of thing.

"I wait in your bungalow," George was saying. "There are plenty of magazines and times passes and before I know it's half past one. So what if you're out rolling in the hay with a neighbor? I don't begrudge a man his fun. Then, this morning I'm eating breakfast when it hits me that there can be a connection between Doc Doane being away all night and Harry Wilde being away. I take a walk and your car's still outside and you're not home and the milk's sitting outside. So I keep walking and find you two lovebirds having breakfast. A romantic scene." He clucked his tongue. "Very romantic."

Lela's hand closed over the edge of the table. She asked the question I didn't have to ask because I knew the answer.

"What do you want, George?"

"Ask your lover-boy. Yesterday I made him a little business proposition. He got mean. I don't think he'll get mean now."

She turned to me. "What does he want?"

"For me to throw basketball games."

"Is that all?" She seemed relieved.

"That's all," I said bitterly. I took a step toward George. "Now it's blackmail on top of bribery. But this time you made a big mistake. You made the offer in front of a witness."

"Me? I never said a word about bribery." He smiled broadly. "But suppose I did? You think I was born yesterday? I'll say it now: I'll pay you off good if you'll play so we can hit the bookies hard. Raise a stink and what comes out? That you crawl into Lela's bed when her husband is away. And if you don't go along with me, I'll see it comes out anyway. How d'you like it?"

Lela pulled her lower lip between her teeth. Her face was all harsh angles. At that moment, she didn't look particularly attractive.

"Talk and be damned!" I said. "And then watch out for me."

He sat looking up at Lela. "You got more sense than this boy scout. That's why I rang you in on this talk. He'll do it for you if you ask him real pretty."

I said: "I'll be damned if—"

"Wait!" She turned away from him; she stood facing me stiffly. "You go now. I'll handle this."

"Listen, Lela," I said. "I'm sorry, but if you think I'll ever consent—"

"No, I guess you wouldn't." She sounded as if she couldn't understand why I should be so unreasonable over so small a matter but that she had to accept it. "George is a heel, and I know how to handle heels."

"Say—" George said indignantly.

"Shut up, heel!" she flung at him without raising her voice. The skin was so tight over her cheekbones that it seemed as if it would split. "Now, go."

I went across the living room and out through the front door. Major met me there. He followed me down the empty road and stayed to keep me company when I sat down to wait on a tree stump.

It was twenty minutes before George Wellman came down the road. He half shambled with his head down and didn't see me until I rose. He stopped walking, and his hand wiped sweat from his mouth.

Hold on," he said nervously. "I was only kidding back there."

"Were you?"

"Sure. After all, Lela's an old pal. Why should I want to queer her with her husband?"

"So there'll be no blackmail?"

"Hell, that was just a gag." He chuckled unconvincingly. "You didn't think I was serious, did you? You two have all the fun you want. It's nothing to me."

I had no idea what Lela had said to him after I had left,

but evidently it had turned the trick. I strode off, in the same direction he would take, but of course not waiting for him. Major tagged along for a short distance, then loped home.

The two bottles of milk delivered to me every other day were on my doorstep in the sun. As I stooped for them, Mr. Hickey sang out, "Good morning, Harry." He was painting in his favorite spot under the maple. I nodded and carried the bottles into the bungalow.

I was hot and tired and thirsty. George Wellman had barged in before I'd had the coffee Lela had served me. The milk I'd brought in would be warm, but there was half a bottle left in the refrigerator. I was drinking the cold milk when somebody rapped on the door.

"Come in."

Mr. Hickey entered briskly. Drinking the milk, I moved from the kitchen to the living room and looked into his dancing eyes.

"How did you find Mrs. Doane?" he asked cheerfully.

I put down the glass. Did everybody in North Set know already?

"Oh, come, don't look so distressed, Harry. It's strictly between us. I haven't mentioned it even to my wife."

"Mentioned what?" I said, trying to maintain the pretense.

"First of all, you shouldn't have been so careless as to leave your door open when you went away."

I hadn't, but George Wellman must have. I should have locked the door, hidden my car, covered my absence like a criminal.

"Last night I attended a meeting of the Town Board," Mr. Hickey was saying. "After it, some of us had a few drinks and considerable talk and it was after two o'clock when I got home. I noticed your door open. I came over to close it and saw that you weren't in. Your car was still here, so obviously you couldn't have gone far. Then a few minutes ago you appeared from the road and took your milk in, and milk deliveries are six o'clock in the morning. It was Mrs. Doane, wasn't it?"

I said dryly: "Would you be disappointed if it wasn't?"

"Harry, Harry," he said sadly, "I tried to warn you against her. And it has to be her. Who else within walking distance has such tremendous appeal? With whom else could you have spent the whole night? No doubt her husband was away overnight."

I finished what was left in the glass. The cold milk was like a solid lump of ice in my stomach.

"Don't flatter yourself," I said. "You didn't drive me to her. It was completely my idea, and hers."

"I drive you to her?" He looked honestly incredulous. "What a notion!"

"All right, maybe it's a screwy notion. What are you after now?"

"Harry, I'm fond of you. I tried to warn you in my own fumbling way. I hardly hoped you'd take my advice. I can still remember my own youth. But that woman! I've painted her, Harry. I think I've seen her soul. Do you know anything about a female praying mantis?"

"You gave me that praying mantis spiel when you showed me that outrageous painting you did of her."

"So I did." His bright, snapping eyes in that pinched face studied me. "What do you propose to do about her—take her away from her husband?"

"Would you mind letting me alone?"

"And if she won't leave her husband, what then?"

"Let me alone!" I yelled. "You're nobody to me. If you have to play with people's lives, use your paint brushes to strip women's bodies naked, but get it into your head that no interfering old busybody—"

I broke off, panting. Mr. Hickey looked as if I had struck him across the face.

"You're right," he said quietly. "An interfering old busybody. It won't happen again."

He walked out with dignity.

I threw myself down on the bed. After a while I stood up and prowled the room. My eyes fell on the basketball. That would be something to do, something to unknot my nerves. I went outside. Mr. Hickey's stool and easel were under the maple, but for the two hours that I shot baskets he didn't appear.

My mind wasn't made up until Bill Hickey's police car pulled up in the driveway next to mine. Occasionally, he came home for lunch. I called to him and he waited for me beside his car.

I told him about the bones Maxine had found somewhere near the knoll. His heavy face remained impassive. "But you're not sure they were human bones," he said when I finished.

"No, not positive."

He slipped into his car and lifted the radio handset from the dashboard and reported to state police zone headquarters that it would take him a couple of hours to investigate a complaint north of North Set. Then he said to me: "I'm going to eat first. Be ready in half an hour."

"I'll be ready."

Chapter Fourteen »»»

BILL HICKEY AND I started the search at the clearing where Maxine had brought me the bones. I thought I remembered she had come from the sumac, but I wasn't sure. We started in at the woods because it was easier; tall oaks kept the ground fairly clear of undergrowth.

We moved slowly in a widening semicircle. A hundred yards from the clearing, we gave up that area because I doubted that Maxine would have strayed so far from me either to find or bury bones. We tried the patch of sumac beside the knoll.

Bill had managed to bring his car to within a quarter of a mile over a murderous, overgrown road that had evidently been unused for years. It was the state's car, so what he did to it didn't bother him. He went back to it and returned with a brush hook and without his gun belt and Stetson. Taking turns with the brush hook, we hacked paths through the sumac.

After a while, he paused to wipe his sweating face and loosen his necktie. A police uniform was no outfit for hard labor.

"Boy, are we getting nowhere slowly!" he complained.

"This is a job for a crew of men. Why not bring them?"

"And look like a fool when we don't find anything?"

"I saw two bones. That ought to be enough reason."

He scowled at me. "You're pretty anxious now—two whole weeks after you saw them."

There was no answer I could make. I took the brush hook from him and set to work. Bill watched me for a minute and then bulled his way ahead through the sumac. The growth was younger near the knoll and I could see his shoulders. I hacked away.

"Harry!" he yelled.

He had completely disappeared from sight. I made my way up the track his body had crushed through the sumac like a miniature bulldozer. He was kneeling some fifteen feet from the rocky slope of the knoll, which at this place rose almost vertically. About him was a small, bare, churned-up area like an island in the sumac.

"Here," he said, pulling something out of the ground. It looked like part of a small plow, but the color was dirty gray and it wasn't metal.

"A hip bone!" I said.

"Yeah." Bill's cheeks had turned the color of the dirt-encrusted bone. "There's a shovel in my trunk. Get it." I ran. The bones had kept for two years and they would keep a minute longer, but I ran to the police car and took the shovel from the trunk and ran back with it.

Bill was scooping up dirt with his hands. Another bone lay beside the first, this one long and thin.

"I'm no expert," he told me, "but it looks like a femur."

"Is that from a leg?"

"Yeah. What were the bones your dog found?"

"A finger and part of an arm—I think. Maxine must have

dug them out from this spot, but I doubt if she'd have buried them in the same place."

He took the shovel from me and dug slowly and carefully. Remembering how small one of the other bones had been, I squatted beside the widening hole and sifted each shovelful through my ringers.

Three or four feet down the shovel struck rock. He scraped it with the edge of the shovel.

"Ledge rock," he said. "It's all ledge around here for God knows how far down, and sometimes it juts up to make a knoll like this one. That's why the grave wasn't dug deeper. You can't build a cellar without blasting. I guess he figured the sumac would grow over it, but the animals kept chewing up the ground to get at"—his voice broke the least bit—"at what he buried here."

I asked: "Does Doane's property run this far?"

"It must, because he bought the old Leonard place, which ran to the other side of this knoll. The land was never good for farming and not much better for pasture. That's why Doane could buy it for a song." He paused and added bleakly: "With the money Alice saved up from teaching."

"And he buried her on his own property to make sure that nobody would ever dig here."

"But animals dug," Bill said. "Maybe his own dogs."

He resumed shoveling, widening and lengthening the hole, scraping clean the rock base of the grave, while I examined the sandy earth he brought up.

"That seems to be all," I said presently, "not counting the two bones Maxine hid somewhere else."

"And no clothes." Bill climbed out of the hole. "Animals would dig and eat and tear, but they wouldn't want the clothes. There should be scraps of clothing."

"He must have buried her naked. Maybe if he had left the body dressed animals wouldn't have touched it." I took out a cigarette. The match shook. "Or maybe, as the stories have it, he let his dogs at her first, then buried what was left."

Bill dropped the shovel and picked up the two bones. Standing with one in each hand, he said: "Two weeks ago you found bones, but you didn't open your yap till today."

"They didn't mean anything at first. Then I started hearing stories about Alice Barton. After a while, I put two and two together. For that matter, what have you been doing about Alice for two years?"

"I didn't have a dog that found bones," he said tonelessly and moved off through the sumac.

I gathered up the brush hook and the shovel and tagged after him. When I reached the clearing, he was sitting on the rock on which I had sat when Maxine had brought me the other two bones. He was running his handkerchief over his heat-flushed face.

I said: "Bill, you were in love with Alice Barton, weren't you?"

He blew his nose and put up the handkerchief. "Who's been talking?"

"I guessed."

He shrugged. "It's no secret in town. We were engaged."

"And then Alice went away on her summer vacation and came back married to Doane."

Bill's powerful hands turned inward on his knees. He said nothing.

"You've never married," I went on. "As far as I know, you haven't even got a girlfriend. Have you been carrying the torch for her all this time?"

He raised his head, and his face was loose and bitter. "Yeah."

"And two years after her marriage she and Doane were suddenly gone, and when he returned he had another wife. Alice hadn't resigned her teaching job; she hadn't sent for her record. Rumors started. But you did nothing—not as a man who loved her or as a cop."

"Stories," he said heavily. "Wacky stories about dogs. Why would a man have killed his wife when he could've divorced her?"

"We know now there must have been a reason."

"Yeah, we know now. But, after all, she was engaged to me and she went off and married Doane without telling me. How did I know she wasn't that kind, going from man to man? How did I know she didn't find another guy in Florida or somewhere and leave Doane for him?"

"So it was a matter of pride?"

"Pride?" he echoed, tasting the word like acid on his lips. "Hasn't a man who's been kicked in the belly a right to be proud? Was I supposed to go whining after her wherever she was?"

"Wasn't anyone in the village anxious to start an investigation?"

"It's a proud little community, Harry. They didn't want any unpleasant notoriety—perhaps a big murder trial, New York reporters, and all that. Officially, they were satisfied with the divorce story."

I stared down at the bones on the ground—all that was left of Kenneth Doane's first wife. It seemed so little.

"Now you know what happened to her," I said, "but you can't prove anything, can you? You can't prove that Alice was buried here or that she was murdered or even that she's dead."

Abruptly he stood up. "I'll prove it."

"But how?"

He picked up the bones and looked bleakly at them. "The identification experts do great things these days. Maybe these are enough for them to tell the age and sex. That'll be a starter."

We returned to his car.

As we drove back, I said: "The bones Maxine found must still be around if other animals didn't get at them, and there were many more bones at the beginning."

"I'm coming back with more men."

"When?"

"This afternoon or tomorrow morning."

"Let me know and I'll help."

He held tightly to the wheel as the car bumped over that caricature of a road. "You stay out of it, Harry. This is strictly police business."

That was all right with me. I was in it as far as I cared to be.

He stopped the car at my bungalow. "Another thing," he said crisply. "Keep this under your hat. Understand?"

"I understand."

He drove on with the bones.

In the bungalow I stripped off my sweaty, grimy clothes. My knees were shaking. For a long time, I stood under a warm shower and for the last thirty seconds I let it pour down on me ice cold. I came out gasping and rubbed myself down. My knees had become steadier, but now something jittered hollowly in my stomach.

Too much was piling up. I was no good at conniving. I couldn't take in stride being the sneaking, surreptitious lover of a married woman and of putting the finger on her husband for murder because I wanted her for myself. I went into the kitchen to make coffee and found that I was out of it. My refrigerator was practically empty; it was five days since I'd gone shopping. I couldn't put it off any longer.

I shaved and dressed. When I was in denims and a T-shirt, I stripped down again to my underwear and put on a white shirt and a necktie and my gray worsted suit. I hadn't got dressed like that since I had left New York.

I drove several miles before it occurred to me that I should have packed a small bag, at least with pajamas and a toothbrush and a razor. It didn't much matter. I had no clear notion where I was going or for how long. All I wanted right now was to get the hell away from everybody and everything in North Set.

Chapter Fifteen »»»

NEW YORK CAN BE very lonely in midsummer, and there is no place at any time where you can be more alone when you want to be. So I was back in the uptown hotel where I had moved when Gale and I had split up, back in the city from which, ironically, Dave Morrison had sent me for rest and peace of mind.

I slept and next day I ate in nearby restaurants and in the evening I walked amid people limp from the heat of pavements that wouldn't cool off. I turned in at a gin-mill for a tall cool drink and kept reordering. But when I was down to the ice of the fourth rum Collins, I told myself that there was no point in getting drunk because next morning I would again be more or less sober, and I had too much pride to go on a prolonged bat. Instead, I went to an air-cooled movie theater.

That was Friday. Saturday I went out of the hotel to find the city emptied for the sweltering weekend. Mid-town Manhattan drooped drowsily. I bought a fresh shirt and underwear and several pairs of socks. What belongings of mine I hadn't taken to North Set were stored in my sister's house in Queens. I ate lunch and reemerged into sunlight with nowhere to go, and all at once I desperately wanted company.

It would have been pleasant to stay with my sister, Rose, and her unobtrusive college professor husband and their two sons, aged fourteen and eleven, who thought I was a very great guy because my name and sometimes my picture appeared in sports pages. But they were spending a month on Cape Cod. Dave Morrison, an easy and sympathetic man to talk to, had no use for New York in the summer; his apartment phone didn't answer. Luke McLarin, the six-eight Gothams' center and my closest friend, was working in a boys' camp in the Adirondacks. There were several old-time girl friends who might be around, and that could include Gale, but it wasn't a woman I wanted and particularly not Gale.

Saturday trickled by, and I was careful not to touch anything stronger than beer for fear that I might not stop.

Sunday morning, as I lay naked on my bed amid scattered sections of the Times, in a hotel room which opened onto a stifling courtyard, I stopped trying to talk myself out of the truth. It was a woman I wanted and nothing else, but only one woman in the world.

Exactly a week ago tonight I had had her for the first time by firelight in my bungalow. She had been free to come to me because her husband had been playing poker. Maybe he played poker every Sunday night, and if so she would be free again tonight. In five hours I could be back in North Set, long before dark.

I didn't go back—not that day. I argued with myself. I said that at any rate it had been my duty to expose a murder and a murderer. Yes, but I hadn't done it out of a sense of duty and I hadn't done it until there had been a wholly selfish reason. I was in New York instead of in North Set because it was not as hard to face myself here as there.

It was hell to have a conscience.

I let Sunday slip away. When I woke up next morning, I knew that I couldn't keep running away. After breakfast I started back.

Chapter Sixteen »»»

WHEN I NEARED Wellman's store, I fought down the temptation to keep going and avoid facing Polly. But, having returned to North Set, how could I avoid facing anybody or anything? Mail had accumulated for me and I would have to get some food if I proposed to stay. I stopped the car.

Mr. Wellman was behind the counter. Nobody else was in the store. That was somewhat of a relief.

"So you're back," he grunted.

That was the difference between New York and North Set: here you couldn't make a move without everybody knowing.

I explained that I had had to go away for a few days. I bought groceries and asked for my mail. He went into the post-office section and a minute later told me through the grilled window that there was nothing for me.

"Somebody must've picked up your mail this morning," he said. "Maybe one of the Hickeys when I wasn't here."

And he looked at me as if about to say more, but he didn't. If the story about the finding of the bones had gone through the village, he would be the first to know here in the center of gossip. I didn't want to discuss the developments, if any, with him. I gathered up my bundle.

Polly Wellman was waiting for me at my car. She must have seen it from an upstairs window.

"Harry!" she cried, and for a moment I was afraid she would throw herself at me.

"Hello," I said, holding the bag of groceries in front of me as if for protection.

Her small hands clenched at her sides. She was lovely, even though she made her eyes and mouth hard. I regretted that it wasn't because of her that I returned.

She seemed to read my mind. "I suppose you couldn't stay away from her!" she flung at me.

It was at the tip of my tongue to ask whom she meant, but there was no point in trying to maintain a pretense.

Her brother George must have told her about me and Lela Doane. That was too bad.

"I'm back because I'm spending the summer here," I said.

"Don't lie. You can't stay away from that woman." Her mouth loosened, started to quiver. She dipped her head. It would be a hell of a note if she burst into tears right here in the open.

"Listen, Polly. I—"

Her head jerked up. "I hate you!" she sobbed and hurried off around the corner of the building.

North Set, the quiet little village where a man could spend a placid summer . . .

I drove on.

I didn't have to unlock the bungalow door because I hadn't locked it when I had left; in the country people seldom bothered with keys. My mail was neatly stacked on the table, the letters in one pile and the newspapers in another. I carried the groceries into the kitchen. When I put the butter and bacon and frozen meat into the refrigerator, I noticed six full bottles of milk. Somebody had taken four of them in from the doorstep.

I returned to the living room and glanced around, frowning, before it struck me that the place was unnaturally gloomy for a bright afternoon. All the window shades were drawn. I certainly hadn't pulled them down before leaving.

"Harry!"

The voice was distant, and it had a breathless quality. I opened the door. Mrs. Hickey was running across her lawn. For a gray-haired woman she did pretty well.

"Harry, you crazy idiot!" she gasped when she was inside. "Why did you give us such a scare?"

"How did I do that?"

"Suddenly disappearing without a word. Gone for days without stopping milk deliveries. I took your milk in."

"Thanks a lot."

Mrs. Hickey leaned against the wall to regain her breath. She pulled a cigarette out of her slacks. I struck a match for her.

"Bill sent out a police alarm for you," she said. "Almost everybody in the village was questioned. What in the world has been going on these last few days?"

"Why the fuss? I spent some time in New York, that's all."

"I tried to tell the menfolk in my family that you're free and single and can get in your car and go anywhere you please, but they acted as if something terrible might have happened to you. They kept whispering to each other and refused to tell me about what. Now why should my husband

and my son treat me like a child? Something is going on."

If she didn't know, obviously nothing sensational had developed concerning the bones. Not publicly, anyway.

"Well, here I am hale and hearty," I said, and to change the subject I waved at the table. "I see my mail as well as my milk was taken care of."

"Polly Wellman brought your mail this morning." Mrs. Hickey blew a thick cloud of smoke between us, and through it her eyes disapproved of me. "It was an excuse to see if you'd returned. She cried her eyes out. Harry, that girl is in love with you."

"I wish she weren't."

"You men! You wish she weren't, but you didn't think of that when you made love to her."

"So her weeping was done on your shoulder," I said dryly.

"A broken-hearted girl has to weep on somebody's shoulder." Angrily she mashed out her cigarette.

From the open doorway, Mr. Hickey said: "Jessica, why don't you let the boy live his own life?"

He must have been listening to at least a part of our conversation. We exchanged nods.

"Nobody can live his own life," she snapped at him. "Whatever you do affects other people. And I don't like the way mysterious things have been happening. Like in this bungalow last night."

"There's nothing mysterious about a sneak thief," Mr. Hickey said.

"This neighborhood hasn't had a robbery in years, and, on top of that, you and Bill being so worried over Harry's disappearance, and then next day when I found—"

"Do you mind letting me in on this?" I broke in.

"I was home alone last night when I saw light in your windows," Mrs. Hickey told me. "Naturally I thought you'd returned. I came over. I had scarcely stepped out of my house when a dog started to bark and the lights went out."

"A dog?" I murmured.

"Yes. When I reached the bungalow the dog was gone. I switched on the light. Nobody was here. The shades were drawn. You didn't leave the shades drawn, did you?"

"I don't remember," I lied.

"I was in here Saturday morning when I took in your milk and I'm positive the shades weren't drawn then. You can see electric light right through them."

Over her gray head my eyes met her husband's, and his had glints in them. He knew as well as I who my caller had been.

I said lamely: "It might have been a tramp and his dog who slipped in to make a meal for himself."

"And built a fire too," she said, "though he couldn't know how long you'd be gone?"

I hadn't noticed before that in the fireplace paper and kindling and logs were all expertly set. It would need only a match to start the fire.

"Oh, that?" I laughed rather inanely. "It was that way when I left."

"No, it wasn't," she declared crisply. "When I took in your milk Saturday, I used that ashtray on the table. It was so full that some of the stubs fell out. I picked them up and emptied the ashtray in the fireplace, and I'd take my oath that there was nothing in there but some wood ashes. Then this morning I saw that." She waved a hand at the fireplace and then fixed me with a stern gaze. "Harry, you're not telling me the truth."

I was fishing for an answer when Mr. Hickey came to my

aid.

"Woman," he said, "I must maintain that a man is entitled to live his own life. Harry is back and we're delighted."

"And if you folks don't mind," I said, "I'd like to get out of these city clothes."

"All right, throw me out," Mrs. Hickey flared.

I assured her that I hadn't meant that at all, but she insisted that I had and that she was fed up with her men and now me lying to her and she hated mysteries anyway, and, shoving a fresh cigarette between her lips, she left without lighting it. By now I should have been used to women misunderstanding or perhaps understanding too well. Mr. Hickey lingered a moment longer to throw me a ribald wink and followed his wife.

I pulled up the shades to let brightness into the bungalow and then stood looking down into the fireplace.

So last night Kenneth Doane had played poker and Lela had come here as she had the Sunday before. She hadn't heard that I was away; not finding me in, she had expected me back any minute and had set the scene. She had pulled the shades and built the fire because she liked firelight—or dim lamplight—for love-making. Then Major, on guard outside, had barked a warning and she had turned off the light and slipped away, perhaps returning after Mrs. Hickey had left and waiting some more.

I could have kicked myself for not having been home last night.

In the early evening Bill Hickey dropped in. I had expected him. He had changed his uniform for white ducks and a sweat shirt. He had an after-dinner cigar in his mouth and a scowl on his face.

"You gave us a fine scare," he growled.

"What did you expect, that Doane had murdered me, too?"

"It could happen. You wouldn't be the first guy knocked off by a jealous husband."

Was there anybody now beside Mrs. Hickey, and probably Kenneth Doane, who didn't know?

"I suppose your father gave you that line," I said.

"He sure did. By Saturday he got worried. He gave me the low-down about you and Mrs. Doane." Bill rolled his cigar on his lower lip. "A guy like Doane—he killed his first wife to be free to marry another woman; so he wouldn't stop at killing a man that other woman was playing around with."

"When I left for a few days, I didn't realize how your father's mind would run."

"My mind ran like that too when I knew what he knew. Your car was gone, but Doane could've hidden it. Your clothes were here—milk, everything. So I went over to have a talk with Doane. Don't get that worried look, Harry. I'm no heel; I didn't let the cat out of the bag. I asked him if he'd seen you in the last couple of days and I had a look around."

"What did you tell Mrs. Doane?"

"I didn't get a chance to tell her anything. That was Saturday afternoon and she was shopping. Yesterday I went back there and nobody was home. Guess they were out for the day. Anyway, that gave me plenty of chance to look over their place." His mouth twisted. "So that's how Mrs. Doane didn't know you weren't here and came to pay you a visit last night. Ma's got a grade-A mystery, but Pa and I know who was waiting for you here."

I said: "Talking of mysteries, did you get anywhere since Thursday? Did you find more bones?"

Bill sagged a little, all the way from the top of his head to his knees. He sat down opposite me at the table and placed his cigar on the ashtray.

"No, we didn't find any more bones. We sent down those two to New York City, where they have a guy in their Missing Persons Bureau who's a whiz at identification. The report came back a little while ago. It said the bones belonged to a woman under thirty about Alice's height and weight."

"But it's no evidence."

"It's evidence enough for me as to what happened to Alice, but it's no evidence in a court of law. So what if a couple of bones of a young woman were found on Doane's property? Even if we could positively prove they were Alice's, we can't prove she was murdered or who murdered her." His fist thumped the table. "There's not a thing except being sure in our own minds, and we can't hurt him with that."

"Have you questioned him yet?"

"What's the good? He'll deny it, and all we'll do is put him on guard. By the way, Harry, keep your lips buttoned. Outside of the police and you and Pa, nobody knows about this. We want to keep it that way while we continue the investtigation."

"Doane claims he divorced Alice in Florida. Can't you check?"

"That's what we're doing. Anyway, the D.A. is. It's mostly in his hands now. He wired Florida to find out if Alice Doane divorced Kenneth Doane two years ago."

"And if it's not on record, what then?"

"We'll be more sure, that's all." He rose and stood chewing his cigar. "I'll get him yet. Some day I'll get him."

He strode to the door and turned. "You should've stayed away, Harry, but I'm a man like you; so I know how it is when a woman gets in your blood. I guess I couldn't keep you two apart even if I had a right to. But be careful, Harry. Tell Mrs. Doane to be the same."

I sat at the table with my hands flat on it and watched the door close behind him.

Later, I went outside and shot baskets until it was too dark to see. I went to bed early, but not to sleep. I lay thinking about how it would have been home last night.

Chapter Seventeen »»»

I DREAMED THAT SHE was undressing in front of the fire. It was smoldering, shedding very little light, and in the closed-in darkness I could distinguish only that a woman was taking off her dress. But there could be no doubt who she was, for of what other woman would I be dreaming, and what other woman would be undressing in my bungalow?

Negligently, she flung the dress on a chair. She took up the poker and prodded the fire. Flames rose gaily crackling, scooping out of deep shadow Lela Doane's high-cheeked, unpainted profile and the curve of a bare shoulder and the rich sweep of hip and flank encased in silk that was so much whiter than the rest of her. She crouched on the hearth as the kindling ignited the logs and she became wholly visible.

The heat drove her back. She straightened and turned her face to the bed, and quickly I shut my eyes.

It wasn't a dream. Realization came gradually, with the languor of full awakening. She had slipped in as I slept and had pulled down the shades and had put a match to the fire she had built last night. She hadn't awakened me because she would want to do that in her own time and in her own way, first setting the scene with firelight and preparing herself, always making some kind of rite of it.

I lay pretending to sleep, in blood-pounding expectancy. There were two small thumps, the second almost over-lapping the first—her shoes kicked off. After that no sound but sparks spitting.

What was delaying her?

I raised my eyelids halfway, looked through the lashes. Two bits of white silk had been flung carelessly on the knitted green dress. She had worn no stockings. As leisurely as if she were alone in her own room, she was removing pins from her hair. The dancing flames threw flickering, volup-tuous radiance over her and turned her tanned skin to gold. She tossed her head and black hair cascaded to her shoul-ders where it shimmered with dark lights. Sensuously she ran her hands over her breasts and around and down to her hips, and I knew that now she would no longer take her time.

Almost before I closed my eyes again she was with me, her mouth spreading moistly over mine, her hands and body urgent, the play completely hers, believing that she was taking me in sleep or in waking to the discovery of her, leaving me no role but clinging compliance to her quick and gasping fury, and almost at once, it seemed, she was through with me and away from me, lying in panting lassitude with our only contact her foot against my leg.

After a while I said: "When does it stop being a game with variations?"

Lela's flickering half-smile was directed at the ceiling. "Didn't you like it?"

"Too much, maybe. Lela, it can't go on like this."

"Do you want it to stop?"

"I want you, all the time. I want you to marry me."

"I have a husband already."

I propped myself up on an elbow, and firelight accentuated the womanliness of her. I said: "You can't keep on having us both."

Her reply was typical. It was no reply except as a commitment for the moment or the hour and it contained no words. She turned to me and pressed me down on my back and lay snuggled with her cheek on my chest and her unhampered hair in my face.

"We haven't much time tonight," she said. "I'll have to leave in a few minutes."

I could just about make out the clock on the chest of drawers. It was a few minutes after one.

"Why did you come so late?" I asked.

"We were already asleep when Kenneth got a phone call. A mare was having trouble giving birth. He left at once. It's twelve miles. He may be back at any time or he may be gone all night."

"And you dressed and walked here."

"I had to after last night. Kenneth was playing poker. But where were you?"

"In New York."

"Oh. And I wanted you, and all day today too. Don't ever do that to me again."

"No," I said. "I'll keep myself on twenty-four-hour call like a stud bull."

Her body stiffened. I expected her to pull away from me, but evidently she decided not to quarrel.

"I waited for you last night," she said. "Then Major warned me that somebody was coming. I thought it was probably you but I hid outside behind a tree to make sure. It was lucky I did because it was Mrs. Hickey. She left in a minute and I waited outside in the dark for two hours. Then this afternoon I drove by and saw your car outside and I knew that if you'd been away you were back."

"And you say you don't like me."

Her torso dug into me. "We can't do without each other, can we?"

"The point is: can you do without your husband?"

"I want you all the time and nobody else, but it isn't so simple. I can't hurt Kenneth."

I laughed harshly. "But it's all right for him to spend all night in New York with Gale."

"He didn't. He's absolutely faithful. And he's like a child. If I left him, he'd be hurt like a child."

"Sure, like a child," I said. "A simple mind running along simple lines. When he wanted you instead of Alice, he—"

I didn't finish. Bill Hickey had insisted I tell nobody.

"He divorced her," she said against my chest. "And I'll divorce him."

"Well, now we're getting somewhere."

"But give me a chance to work it out. I'll have to break it to him gradually. He'd be too hurt if I told him about you. I'll tell him I no longer care for him and want a divorce, and I'll go away—to Reno perhaps—and get it, and then we'll be together all the time."

I thought that now at last she might say she loved me, that at least she could call me by some endearment or say my name, which, on her lips, would be like a term of affection. But she lay silent, and in the end I was the one who whispered huskily: "Lela, I love you."

And, after all, her response was more satisfying and more eloquent than words. She shifted her body up for her mouth to reach mine and I felt her tongue on the inside of my lips.

This time it was slow and blending and pervading and a complete sharing.

When she was dressing, the fire had died to embers. She was a shadow among shadows. I watched her from the bed, and for the first time in months I had a sense of well-being. Soon there would be no necessity to sneak to each other under cover of darkness and pull down window shades and lock doors and watch clocks. She would be all mine and she loved me. She hadn't said it in words, but her ardor said so and what she intended to do, and acts didn't lie or mutter conventional phrases of love because they were expected.

In pajamas, I walked to the door with her.

She threw back her head for my kiss. I gripped her shoulders. Against her lips I said: "When will you tell him?"

"I don't know."

"Tonight? Tomorrow?"

"Give me time. I'll have to do it my own way."

"All right."

I unlocked the door and pulled it open and she slipped out.

Soft light streamed down from a white half-moon. Holding the door partly open, I watched her move away. She didn't have to use her flashlight. A gray shape appeared in my line of vision. Lela touched Major's head and walked on down the driveway.

I started to close the door and paused. Major wasn't following her. He was looking back at something at the side of the bungalow. I felt my throat constrict.

Lela had reached the road. She uttered a low whistle. The dog hesitated as if in indecision, then trotted after her. Lela disappeared behind trees that flanked the road.

It was nothing, I assured myself as I closed the door. If

there were anybody nearby, Major would have barked a warning as he had last night when Mrs. Hickey had approached. But the front window drew me. I pulled up the shade and saw another shape on the driveway.

In the back of my mind, I must have known that the one person whose presence Major would accept without an uproar was his master.

Kenneth Doane, looking immense in moonlight in a crumpled white-linen suit, followed his wife. In a moment he, too, was out of sight behind the trees.

Chapter Eighteen »»»

I RAN ALONG THE empty road. I had lost two precious minutes: one as I had remained dazed and guilty and uncertain after he had disappeared from sight, then another minute to strip off my pajamas and throw on clothes.

They couldn't be far ahead. They were both walking; I should catch up to them within less than half a mile.

Then what? He had already murdered one wife. Maybe all I was doing was racing to be murdered along with his second wife.

I wondered if he had a gun.

My lungs were catching fire, but I didn't dare stop running.

If he had a gun and proposed to use it, wouldn't the time have been when he had stood outside the bungalow listening to us inside? The door had been locked, but he could have smashed a window. Or he could have let us have it at the moment when she had stepped out and I had been exposed in the doorway. So he had no gun or didn't plan to use it. Instead, he was stealthily following her home.

He was experienced in murder; the cautious way had paid off before. When he had followed her back to their isolated house, he would do to her what he had done to Alice Barton and then say she had left him.

Was I scaring myself with ghosts conjured up by gossip and a couple of bones and my own sense of guilt? I knew nothing except that I couldn't leave her alone with him, and I had no idea what I would do and say when I reached them.

But where were they? I should have caught up to them by now.

From around a sweeping bend I heard a car engine sputter into life. I stopped, gasping for air. In the stillness of the night, I could hear gears grind. That would be the worn transmission of the station wagon. Through the trees, indirect light filtered from the far part of the curve—the edges of receding headlights.

I sprinted. When I rounded the curve, there was no car or person on the road.

Doane must have parked his station wagon here and walked the rest of the way to my bungalow so that he could approach silently and warn Major not to give his presence away. And here, half a minute ago, Lela had got into the car with him.

Maybe not willingly. Maybe she was already dead.

For a moment I debated whether to return for my car. But I wouldn't gain much time and it would have been maddening to retrace my steps. I went on, running again until a stitch in my side slowed me down. I had to walk the rest of the way. For the first time, I put on my flashlight.

When I neared the Doane house, I figured that they were some ten minutes ahead of me. All the tragedy in the world could occur in less time.

No dogs rushed out to me or even raised their voices from the barn. I had been afraid of them. Now, as I turned off the road, a little of the tension left me, but only a little.

The station wagon was there and the house was dark.

It struck me that I had made a terrible mistake. It wasn't the station wagon I had heard. They hadn't come here after all. He had taken her into the woods on the way and it was too late.

With the doused flashlight swinging like a club in my hand, I moved to the station wagon and felt the radiator.

It was warm. I pulled breath into my still burning lungs.

They were here then. But where?

I looked about slowly and noticed the light in the living room window. The bulb evidently was dim and far from the window; with moonlight on the pane, at the first brief glance the vague glow hadn't looked like an inside light. It told me nothing. Quite possibly he or she had left it on earlier that night.

I went to the porch. My foot was raised to the first step when some-thing like a dark mist whisked by the window. And there was a half-muted sound—a whisper, a sigh, a rustle—I couldn't tell except that it came from the house. Somebody or something was in the living room.

Cautiously I placed my raised foot back on the ground. These sagging porch steps, I knew from experience, would creak. I moved around the corner of the house to the two living room windows facing the road. A dogwood tree, low and heavy with leaves, grew close to the windows; you had to be up close before you noticed the diffused glow. I straightened up at one of the windows.

The shade of a floor lamp was tilted horizontally like a baby spotlight, its ray thrown away from the windows and focused on Lela Doane, who was whirling in a huge black veil.

It took time for me to get it, to believe my eyes, to convince myself that what I saw was real. I had expected her dead or in imminent danger or at least in a violent quarrel, but here she was serenely dancing for her husband, who a short while ago had watched her come from my bungalow.

The low-power lamp spread mellowness over her like firelight in my bungalow. She wore nothing but that black veil swirling and writhing about her, and through it her body glimmered riper and more naked than nakedness.

Doane sat sunk in an armchair, his hands clutching the chair's arms, his chest, straining shirt and linen jacket, rising and falling. His blond hair was tousled like a small boy's, but his face had become loose and sodden. His head was very still except for his eyes shifting in their sockets to follow her movements. And two of the dogs were there also, the German shepherds, Major and his mate, their muzzles on their extended forepaws, and, like their master, not taking their eyes from her.

There was no music. Her body provided its own rhythm. She did not move about much on bare and silent feet or throw herself in crude acrobatics. Her torso rippled, and through the large-meshed veil splashes of light intimately caressed her. She swayed sinuously. Her lips were parted in a smile that was like the dance—subtle and sultry and hypnotic.

Doane stirred. His massive chest rose as if to bring up breath to say something. The veil whirled and came to rest on her shoulders like a cape. He subsided with only his hungry eyes alive.

This was a ritual of sheer sexuality, like her unhurried build-up for love-making with me. Where would this end? Would she soon throw herself, naked and eager, at her husband?

I told myself that I should go away because this was indecent spying, and I told myself that I still must not leave her alone with him. Perhaps I could not have torn myself from the window at any rate. Like Doane—and the dogs, too—I was held in a kind of trance by what she was doing with her veil and her body.

Suddenly, I heard the voices of the two dogs that were not in the house.

I spun from the window. They were coming at me. They must have been loose and away and had just returned. I saw them charge past the station wagon, and I ran.

Probably if I had stood my ground they wouldn't have touched me, but they would have exposed me spying at the window. I was anxious to get to the road and pretend that I had just arrived. My flight showed them that I feared them, and they gave chase.

The red setter caught me on the road. He hooked his fangs into the fleshy part of my leg. I used my flashlight as a club. The first blow glanced off his skull and he held on. Then out of the darkness the chow hurled herself at me. I went down on both knees. The setter released my leg, but now I was occupied with trying to keep the chow from my throat.

Other dogs barked. A man shouted: "Down! Down, I say!"

In their savage frenzy, they didn't immediately obey their master. Doane had to pluck the chow off me and hurl her away.

"Quiet!"

Gradually their voices stilled. Doane was helping me up to my feet. This, on top of the long run, was a bit too much; I thought I would be sick over him. I managed to hold it down. I stood groggy, unsteady, clinging to him on the moonlit road while the four dogs prowled restlessly about us.

"Having her in your bungalow wasn't enough," Doane said between his teeth. "You had to come here."

"I-I—"

Fog clouded my brain. No words seemed the right ones. I felt blood trickle down my leg.

Without warning Doane drove his fist, into my jaw. I staggered. He hit me in the cheek and I went down, slumping once again to my knees. "Let him alone," Lela said quietly. Light covered me. I fought my head up. I blinked into the direct glare of a flashlight. She dipped it and, behind it, I saw her stand barefooted in her calico wrapper. A shotgun rested in the crook of her right arm, and her finger was on the trigger.

"I'll kill him!" Doane's voice was a ragged sob. "I saw him run from the window. He was watching you dance." He laughed crazily. "That wasn't the first time he saw you naked, but it'll be the last."

He stepped toward me with fists that looked the size of basketballs.

"Let him alone," Lela repeated.

Over his shoulder, he glanced at her and for the first time, it seemed, he noticed the shotgun.

"Lela, for God's sake, you wouldn't!"

"Then don't make me," she said tonelessly.

I struggled up to my feet. My torn leg wobbled under me.

Nobody spoke. We stood on the road, surrounded by the dogs, who were now as still as we, and Doane and I stared at the gun which she held competently pointed at his chest.

Her skin was so tight over her cheek-bones that it seemed about to split and her eyes receded darkly in shadowed sockets. The scant wrapper hung loosely, partially away from her breasts and thighs; she had had no time to tie it tight.

I found my voice. "Look," I said, "can't we straighten this out without killing each other?"

Slowly Doane turned his head to me. "I don't know," he muttered.

"I know what went on between you and Gale last Wednesday night in New York," I flung at him. "So don't act so damn holy yourself."

"You're wrong. I didn't—I never—" He was stammering in denying his own guilt, and to an extent he had now put himself on the defensive.

"I bet you didn't," I sneered.

Doane looked again at Lela—not so much at her as at the gun. "Lela, what are we going to do?" he asked brokenly.

"Wait for me in the house."

"No. You come with me."

"I'll join you in a few minutes. I want to talk to him."

"You'll come right in?" he pleaded.

"Yes."

He took three steps and paused beside her and said emptily: "Tie your robe, Lela."

With the hand that held the flashlight she pulled the wrapper closer about her. Doane moved on. He had become merely pathetic.

Three of the dogs followed him. Major faithfully remained with his mistress.

We didn't speak until lights went on in the house. Then she said: "You fool! Did you have to come here?"

"I saw him follow you. I had to protect you."

"I told you not to worry about me. He'll never harm me. But you—he might have killed you."

"Thanks for saving my life," I said dryly. "I'd like to do the same for you."

Her robe had fallen loose again, more open than before. She ignored it.

"Did you see me dance?" she asked.

"Yes."

"I had to. He was terribly upset, of course. Somebody had told him about us."

"George Wellman?"

"Kenneth said it was a woman's voice. A few days ago somebody called him on the phone and told him and hung up. He didn't believe it; there's so much malicious gossip. Then tonight he came home sooner than I expected and he found me gone and he went to your bungalow and saw me."

"Sooner or later it was bound to happen."

"I suppose so," Lela said tiredly. "As soon as we were home, I danced for him. It—it seems to make him forget everything but me. It makes him want me very much."

"I know. I saw it." I shifted all my weight from my wounded leg. "And after dancing you would have given yourself to him."

She retreated into one of her silences. Light appeared in two upstairs windows.

I said: "You can't go back to him now."

"I must."

"This is the time to make the break."

"Not tonight."

"Why not tonight? You said you needed a chance to let him know. All right, he knows."

"But I can't run out like this in the middle of the night. I need more time."

"Time for him to kill you?"

"Don't be silly."

"You keep saying he won't harm you, but you had to dance like that to keep him under control. Will he still be under control when you go back to him tonight? And how will he feel tomorrow?"

"I know him. I'll be safe."

I put my hands on her. Through the wrapper her smooth flesh felt cold.

"Listen," I said. "He murdered his first wife."

She pulled away from me. "Don't come so close. He can see us from the house, and there's no sense irritating him more."

"Did you hear what I said? He murdered Alice."

"Gossip!" she snorted.

"Last week police found bones in a grave at the foot of the knoll. They're the bones of a woman Alice's age and height and weight."

"You're just telling me this to make me go with you."

"I swear it. Call up Bill Hickey and ask him."

She leaned on the shotgun.

"No," she said as if to herself. "Those men were looking for a lost child."

"What men?"

"Last week—Friday, I think—Kenneth saw some men from an upstairs window at the far end of our property. He went out to them. Some were policemen. They said a child had wandered from home and they were searching for it."

"They were looking for more bones. They don't want him to know until they have more evidence, but they know he murdered Alice."

She stood with shoulders huddled, bare-legged and childlike in pale light.

Her head came up. "I don't believe it. Kenneth is so gentle."

"The way he was gentle with me just now? He was so gentle you brought a shotgun to save me from him."

"That's different. You're a man and men fight over women. But he—he loves me. No matter what I do, he'll love me."

I said bitterly: "If you keep dancing for him."

"Harry, please."

Once, after we had spent the whole night together, I had asked her to say my name and she had, but she hadn't uttered it again until now. On her lips it sounded somehow more intimate than even our love-making.

"What is it?" I said. "Don't you care enough for me?"

"I don't want you hurt or dead. Can't you see what will happen if I go with you now? He'll come after us. There's another gun in the house—a rifle."

"I thought he was so gentle," I taunted.

"Yes—with me. But if I go now with you in the middle of the night, it will be different." She moved toward me, but not all the way. "I can work it out. Give me time. I can make him see reason."

"Are you going to sleep with him tonight?"

"Don't ask that."

"Are you?"

"I'll try not to. He's had a terrible shock tonight. He's not himself. By morning it will be different. Come for me in the morning and we three will talk it over like civilized people."

Wearily I nodded. I had seen the man watch her dance and I had seen him crushed and pathetic as he had walked away from us a few minutes ago. He was waiting for her to come back to him because that was all that mattered. I could appreciate how he felt.

Blood was flowing down to my sock. I thought that I would keel over if I stood there talking much longer.

"Till tomorrow then?" she said, anxiously watching my face.

"All right."

She touched my arm lightly and moved away. Major went with her.

I found my flashlight on the road where it had fallen when I had been attacked by the dogs. It still worked. I sat down at the side of the road and pulled up the left leg of my pants and with my pocket handkerchief wiped off clotting blood. The cloth had protected me somewhat; the fangs had just barely broken the skin. There was more blood than pain.

A dog barked distantly. Probably Maxine. Maxine, who in a way had started all this.

I remained seated in the damp grass at the side of the road. I looked at my watch: close to four. Soon dawn would come. I sagged with fatigue.

Every downstairs light on that side of the house went out. The one that remained on upstairs would be in the master bedroom—their bedroom.

Don't think about it. Come back tomorrow and take her away from here and start from scratch together, clean and honest. I pushed myself up to my feet. Anyway, the leg wasn't stiff.

I dragged myself home. My bed felt as if it still retained the warmth of her body.

Chapter Nineteen »»»

I AWOKE FROM FIVE hours of fitful sleep. I felt like something the cat had dragged in.

A shower washed cobwebs from my head. I examined the dog bite which I had doctored before going to bed. It was somewhat sore to the touch, but it looked all right. I could be sure that a dog owned by a veterinary had been inoculated against rabies. I dabbed more iodine on it. I had one other memento from last night: a dark bruise over my cheekbone where his fist had smacked me.

She had told me to come for her in the morning. By twenty minutes after ten, I was dressed and drinking coffee.

The coffee floated in my hollow stomach. That was where tension always hit me. I felt somewhat the way I did before an important basketball game.

I would drive openly up to the house—and then what? Leave it to Lela. She had known what she was doing last night after he'd caught her here; she'd know what to do this morning. By now she had perhaps induced him to agree to let her go off with me without fuss and without contesting a divorce.

All the same, I wished I had a gun that would fit into my

pocket.

I took a steak knife out of the kitchen cabinet drawer. I balanced it on my palm and then put it back. I lit a cigarette and drew smoke down to my lungs and went out to my car.

The sky was low and dull and oppressive, and the air was sticky. The weather fitted the way I felt. I drove at normal speed.

Again, like last night, the dogs raised no clamor at my approach. In a few seconds I saw why. They were busy feeding in the paddock. Kenneth Doane stood outside the paddock watching them.

Only his head turned when I pulled in behind the station wagon. I got out of the car and stood beside it and looked at the house. There was no sign of her. I didn't know what to do—honk the horn or call out to her or wait where I was.

"What do you want now?" Doane said thickly.

Across twenty feet of space we faced each other. He didn't look hostile—only fatigued and bitter. He wore no shirt and I noticed that when the blond Adonis didn't hold himself in he showed quite a bit of belly at the belt buckle. His face was puffy and his eyes were haggard.

"Where's Lela?" I said.

His mouth became sullen. "She's gone."

"Gone where?"

"I thought she'd gone with you," he muttered and turned his back to me. And, as if his interest in the subject had ended completely and for all time, he watched his dogs feed.

The dogs were tearing at something raw and red and bloody. They were fifty feet in from the fence and surrounding their food and I couldn't quite see what it was.

"Listen," I said through a tight throat, "I haven't seen her since last night. Did she tell you where she was going?"

"When I woke up this morning she wasn't here," he muttered without looking at me.

He was lying. She couldn't have traveled any distance without the station wagon. She had told me to come for her this morning, and if she had gone anywhere it would have been to me.

I stood against the paddock fence, but still the dogs were between me and what they were eating. It was too quiet here, too ominous. Doane continued to ignore me.

I strode to the house.

I had reached the porch steps when I heard his voice. "Where do you think you're going?"

"To look for her," I said.

With his head lowered between his shoulders, he moved toward me heavy-footed.

"Get off my property," he shouted.

"Not until I have a look in the house."

"Get off!"

There was no point in arguing. I knew what would happen, and that would be all right. I took another step toward the house. He grabbed my arm, yanked me around, and swung at my face.

This wasn't like last night when I had been dazed by the dogs' attack. I was ready. I yanked my head sideways and took the blow grazingly on my temple. He had started it now, as he had last night, and for some reason I wanted it that way. And I wanted what followed. At close range I drove my fist into his bare midriff. He was soft as mush there. He grunted and as I stepped back I slammed an uppercut into his jaw. I felt my knuckles split.

Already he was panting, wavering, and I knew I had him.

We fought, and the dogs were our audience. They left off feeding and made the morning hideous with their growling and hurled themselves at the high wire fence. I was lucky they weren't loose.

Doane outweighed me by at least thirty pounds, but his magnificent build was a fraud. He was flabby; I was a trained athlete, quick with my hands and feet, and more or less in condition. He shouldn't have boxed me. He should have got his arms around me and used his superior weight and strength, but instead he tried to slug. He hadn't much punch for his size and he was slow. I danced around him, cutting his face with jabs, letting him have it again and again in the midriff, which seemed to be his most vulnerable spot.

He crumpled slowly, sinking, and sat with his face in his hands. I stood over him, trembling with exhaustion. "Now I'm going into the house," I gasped and waited for his answer.

He wobbled up to his feet. He tried to look at me, but his eyes wouldn't focus. His face was a bloody mess. Teetering, he pushed his hands at me. He was helpless, but this wasn't a sporting match. I swarmed all over him with my fists. He was out cold before he hit the ground.

I bent over him. He was breathing low and ragged through his slackly open mouth. The skin of his ribs, battered purple, twitched. I went into the house.

In the living room, reaction set in. I leaned sobbing for breath against the wall. My face ached. I hadn't by any means escaped punishment. I sucked blood from my split knuckles—his blood as well as mine.

Outside the dogs were quiet. The stillness of the house was sheer terror. I remembered the sense of fright the last time I had stood here, last Wednesday night when the house had been dark and I hadn't yet known that she was waiting for me upstairs. But then there had been only doubt as to where she was. Now . . .

I pulled myself up the stairs by the banister.

The door to their bedroom was open. On the bed, a blanket was in crumpled disorder. Both pillows had obviously been slept on. That meant nothing; she had told me that last night she had got out of bed to come to me. And if later she had gone back to bed with him, that still revealed nothing about what had happened between then and now.

A handbag was on the dresser—green leather. I found in it among the usual junk a wallet containing her driver's license and seventeen dollars. She might have other handbags, but not another wallet. She would have taken it.

She hadn't gone anywhere.

Easy. Make sure.

I opened drawers. Two of them contained his stuff. Two held her underwear and nightgowns and stockings. In a corner of one was a little pottery box full of jewelry. Most of it consisted of cheap necklaces and bracelets and earrings, but there was an amethyst brooch with small pearls around it that a woman wouldn't want to leave behind.

I examined the closet. His suits and her dresses were mingled on the hanger bar. He had very little and she not much more. I recognized the green knitted dress and the gingham dress and the evening gown I had seen only in Mr. Hickey's painting. There were two other dresses, and there were skirts and slacks and blouses. I had no way of knowing if all her clothes were here, but, if she had left of her own will not to return, wouldn't she have taken at least some of the clothes in this closet and in the dresser?

A pair of Doane's baggy pajamas was on a chair on top of

his linen suit. There was no nightdress of hers in sight, though earlier last night she had been in bed.

Where, by the way, was her calico wrapper?

Was she wearing it still and nothing else, or not even the wrapper, buried naked the way he had evidently buried his first wife?

Stop scaring yourself.

No, I was facing it. Last night I had left her here to die.

My knees wobbled so that I could hardly stand. The fight with Doane hadn't weakened me that much. I shuffled out to the hall and braced myself against the wall for a moment and then opened the door.

This was the room where we had spent a night together. The bed was made, covered by a faded spread. She hadn't come in here to spend the rest of the night away from him.

I stood at the window. The branches of a tree were in the way; I could hear the dogs snarling, but I couldn't see them. Below the window, Doane remained unconscious.

My throat burned with dryness. I stopped off in the bathroom for a drink of water. My face in the medicine-chest mirror wasn't any prettier than Doane's except that there was no blood. A mouse was developing under my right eye. I let water run and washed the blood off my knuckles and dried my hands on a towel.

Downstairs in the living room, I found the black veil. I hadn't noticed it the first time I had passed through. It lay fragile and transparent beside the leg of the couch. She must have tossed it there last night when she had rushed to get the wrapper and the shotgun.

I moved on into the kitchen and there was the calico wrapper. It hung over the back of a wooden chair.

I stared at it. Why would she have taken it off in the kitchen and then gone naked from here? No, she'd brought her clothes down here and dressed. But in the kitchen?

Why this speculating? I knew the answer, didn't I? She hadn't taken the wrapper off herself. He had taken it off her—afterward—and left it here.

I looked through the screen door and saw that Doane was sitting up. Slowly he shook his head from side to side, as if testing his neck muscles. Likely his next move would be to go for one of his two guns, the shotgun or the rifle she had mentioned. I hadn't come across either. I hadn't looked in all the closets or in the attic or the cellar.

I had found enough. From here on in, it was in the hands of the police.

He was starting to rise. If he opened the paddock gate and let out the dogs, I'd be in a pretty bad way. I hurried out through the kitchen door.

He was halfway up when he saw me. He sank down again and stared blearily at me for a moment; then his head dipped as if too great a weight for his shoulders.

In the paddock the dogs lay about sluggishly with full stomachs. Maxine barked several times in her kennel and subsided.

Leaning against the paddock fence, I could now make out what the dogs had been feeding on. It wasn't anything like a human body—more like the hind quarter of a horse, probably another section of the carcass I had seen them make a meal of a couple of weeks ago.

"Now get out of here!" Doane said in a voice so thick that it was like speaking through blood.

I spun around. He could barely stand upright, but he was holding a murderous crowbar raised.

"Haven't you done enough?" he sobbed. "You made her

leave me."

I felt cold all over. It wasn't so much fear of the crowbar. He was so weak that I could manage to keep away from him. But there was something pathetic about him as he wobbled there—tragic and not quite sane.

Had the second murder completely unhinged his mind?

"Get out of here," he sobbed. "Get out, get out."

And there were tears in his eyes and he sniffled through his ruined nose.

Cautiously I skirted around him. His body turned with me, but he didn't come at me with the crowbar, didn't move his feet.

I got into my car. I should have phoned the police from here while he had been unconscious, but in five minutes I could do so from my bungalow.

Whatever he had done to Lela couldn't be undone now.

I backed my car out to the road and as I shifted gears I looked back. He had dropped the crowbar. With the back of a hand, he was wiping blood from his mouth.

Chapter Twenty »»»

THE VOICE IN state police headquarters told me that Sergeant Hickey was cruising in his patrol car.

"Would you get in touch with him right away?" I said.

"What's it about?"

I paused. "A murder."

The news didn't excite the voice. "Who's this speaking?"

"My name's Harry Wilde."

"Just a minute, please." I could hear the buzzing voices of at least two people speaking away from the phone. Then the voice returned. "Are you the Harry Wilde who led Sergeant Hickey to part of a skeleton in North Set?"

"That's right."

"You say you have additional information?"

It could be called additional information.

"Plenty," I said. "This is urgent. I'm in my bungalow. Sergeant Hickey knows where it is."

"Right. Wait there for him."

I hung up and sucked my split knuckles. I went into the bathroom and bathed my bruised face. Then I went out to the road to wait. My leg muscles didn't cease quivering.

Bill Hickey must have been cruising nearby, for he arrived before I had finished my second cigarette. He came at a fast clip; brakes started to squeal as the police car passed his own driveway. He stopped beside me. I opened the door.

"Holy cat!" he said. "What meat grinder did you put your face into?"

I sat beside him and showed him my knuckles. "You should see Kenneth Doane's face." I dropped my cigarette through the window and gulped air. "He killed Lela."

Bill shot me a quick glance and put the car into gear. When he was moving at high speed, he said: "He caught you two together, huh?"

"Yes. Last night. But that wasn't why we had the fight."

"Damn it, didn't I warn you?" His mouth twisted. "Okay, I knew it wouldn't do any good. You knew the score. Let's have it."

I began at the end and worked back and skipped about and sounded wild and incoherent to myself. But he got enough of it to realize that there was no need to hurry and that it would be better for him to have it all before we reached there. He stopped the car.

"Hold it," he said. "You didn't see her body or any sign of murder."

"I saw enough. She was expecting me to come for her this morning. If she'd decided she couldn't wait, she'd have phoned me or walked to my place."

"Could be she was fed up with both of you."

"All right," I said. "But why didn't she take her clothes and her expensive brooch and her wallet? Why was her wrapper in the kitchen? Why didn't she drive the car at least to the Fort Able station?"

He nodded gravely. "Alone, none of that would mean so much, but after last night . . ."

He drove on.

The knuckles of both my hands were at my mouth. I said against them: "And last night I went home and left her there to be killed."

"Cut it out, Harry."

"I knew something would happen. You said it yourself: the second murder is easy. But I let her talk me out of protecting her."

"Let me tell you something," Bill said gently. "You can't protect people who don't want it or who don't believe they're in danger. What could you have done?"

"I could have called the police."

"And what could we have done? We can't force a woman not to spend a night with her husband, and he wasn't disobeying any law." A queer sound that was not quite a laugh trickled through his nostrils. "Yeah, he didn't disobey any law but murder Alice. We'd never have pinned it on him. But this one, by God!"

His big hands opened and closed on the wheel.

We heard the dogs when we entered the side road. They were howling rather than barking, and it seemed to me that there was a lonely, plaintive quality in their voices. Did they know their mistress was dead?

As the car swung off the road, I saw that they were out of the paddock, but they didn't rush up to us. All four were huddled at the barn door, and near them Kenneth Doane lay face down on the ground.

Oddly, his hair no longer looked blond, but I had only a glimpse before the station wagon cut off my view of him.

I said: "He must have passed out again after I—"

Bill yanked up the hand brake and without cutting the engine slammed out of the car. All I could see of Doane were his legs, one extended at a sprawled angle and one bent at the knee. The dogs had become quiet. My heart thumped.

I got out of the car. Past the side of the station wagon, I saw Bill bending over Doane. The dogs watched him without menace, as if something had completely cowed them. I moved around the station wagon and stopped abruptly.

The back of Doane's head was gone.

Bill, still kneeling, stared at me over his shoulder. He said bleakly: "So all you used were your fists!"

I wet my lips. "Is he dead?"

"What do you think? They don't live with their skull smashed into their brain by a crowbar."

My eyes shifted on past Bill and the dead man and came to rest on the long black crowbar on the bare ground. Even from where I stood I could see on it dark blood and bits of skin and flesh.

"Listen," I said. "That's the crowbar he threatened me with to make me leave. He dropped it when I got into my car. Then somebody . . ."

My voice faded as Bill rose. His right hand crossed to the gun on his left hip, touched the stock, then came away.

"Where's Mrs. Doane?" he asked.

"I told you I don't know what he did with her."

"Maybe you found her dead. Anyway, you were sure he'd murdered her—the way he'd murdered Alice. And you killed him."

For the last minute, I had seen that coming.

"No," I muttered.

"I'm sorry, Harry." He glanced toward the knoll, and his jaw muscle bulged, quivering. "He deserved what he got, but it's not for me to say. I'm a cop."

"I tell you he was alive when I left him."

"You tried to be too smart," Bill said, as if angry at me for having botched it. "You should've gone home and let somebody else find the body. It might've been days, and then—" He scowled. "You're under arrest."

He pulled out a pair of handcuffs.

I didn't care. I was too empty inside, too emotionally and physically exhausted. A man could reach a point where he didn't much care what happened after that.

"I won't run away," I said.

He looked into my face. "No, I guess not." He went to his car and pulled out the radio handset and stood watching me as he spoke into it.

In her kennel in the paddock Maxine started to yelp shrilly. The other dogs stirred nervously, growling.

"Yeah," I heard Bill report, "I have him right here."

Chapter Twenty-one »»»

DISTRICT ATTORNEY James Berwick was a restless, ener-
getic man no older than myself. He had taken office in Jan-
uary and this was the first case he could get his teeth into.
He was seldom still; he bounced around even when I was
telling my story, and his questions were hurled at me like
missiles.

He also went in for heavy-handed psychology. He had
me sit on a wooden kitchen chair in the middle of the Doane
living room, facing Mr. Hickey's painting of Lela Doane
above the fireplace. With her image before me, I was supposed to break down and confess. After an hour or so, Berwick began to act as if I weren't playing the game fair by
sticking to my story.

Somebody called him from upstairs. He tore up the
stairs two at a time. A morose deputy sheriff with a gun on
his hip kept me company. I listened to the sounds outside
the house.

Maxine, excited by the unusual activity, was barking
incessantly. I hadn't heard the Doane dogs since shortly
after the police had started to arrive. Cars kept coming and
going.

Berwick charged down the stairs. "Now we have you cold, Wilde. We found blood in the bathroom basin."

"Of course," I said. "I washed my hands when I was upstairs looking for Mrs. Doane. You can see what happened to my knuckles. They were bleeding."

"Are you sure you didn't wash off his blood?"

"Some of it may have been his." My voice was hoarse with fatigue. "I hit him a number of times after his nose started bleeding. I think his mouth bled too."

"And his head," Berwick snapped. "The coroner tells me those head wounds of his bled plenty. And spurted. Blood must've got all over you."

"Sure, and missed my clothes and hit only my hands."

He scowled at me. He didn't approve of that answer or any other I had given him. He bounced to the screen door and stood there looking out.

"What about Mrs. Doane?" I asked.

"I'm waiting for you to tell me. What about her?"

"Are you looking for her body?"

"We look for everything. Sergeant Hickey and some of his men are going through this area with the Doane dogs on leashes. Maybe the dogs will find her."

I nodded. "That big shepherd was especially devoted to her. He'll find her even if—if Doane buried her deep."

Berwick squirmed his shoulders as if something were itching him. Then he dashed through the screen door.

A few minutes later another deputy came in. He and the one who was guarding me took me outside. A blanket was spread over Doane's body. Berwick and a state policeman with a gold badge stood nearby talking. At the moment, nobody else was in sight. The deputies herded me into a car and drove me to the jail in Fort Able.

There were four cells in the basement of the red-brick county building. I became the only occupant. The furnishings consisted of a cot and a chair from which paint was peeling and a bucket. Close to the ceiling there was a narrow barred window only a couple of feet above the outside ground level.

After a while the morose deputy returned with a tray of watery soup, undercooked spaghetti, overboiled coffee. But it was food and I surprised myself by being hungry. And when I stretched out on the cot, I managed to sleep.

Toward evening, the deputy awoke me. He led me up two flights of stairs to the district attorney's office.

Berwick sat behind his desk. Almost affably he waved me to an upholstered and quite comfortable chair. A skinny, middle-aged woman sat at a smaller desk, a short-hand notebook open and a pencil sharpened. The deputy stood with his shoulders against the door.

I said: "Did you find her?"

"Not yet." Berwick himself didn't bounce, but he bounced a pencil on the desk blotter. "We went over every inch of the house and the barn and the grounds. She's not buried there."

"Then Doane played it safer this time. He took her body away in his station wagon and buried it far from his place."

"Possibly. Now tell me exactly what took place. All of it this time."

So I went over it all once more while the stenographer wrote it down for the record.

When I finished, Berwick complained: "You haven't changed your story."

"The truth doesn't change."

He sat back and smiled. "I've found out a thing or two

about you, Wilde. You're a big man in sports. You've an excellent reputation. A fine war record. People who know you speak highly of you. As for your affair with Mrs. Doane"—he shrugged—"it could have happened to anybody. I never saw her in person, but I saw that painting of her in her home and I can understand how a man can lose his head over her."

His technique had changed. He was using soft soap.

"You were aware of the evidence that pointed to the fact that Doane had murdered his first wife," he went on. "Indeed, we're grateful to you for your assistance there. I regret, however, that we wouldn't have been able to pin it on him except in the unlikely event that additional evidence was discovered."

I said: "By the way, did you ever learn if he and Alice had been divorced in Florida?"

"There was no such divorce. It's quite certain that Alice never left North Set. Let me resume. You were in a position to believe that he had murdered his first wife. When you returned this morning and found that his second wife had disappeared, you were justified in assuming that he had done the same to her. You had a fight with him. Up to that point, I'm inclined to think you're telling the truth."

I found myself shifting to the edge of the chair.

"Doane was bigger and stronger than you," he said. "He was getting the best of the fight."

"No. I was faster and in better condition and had more of a punch. I knocked him out."

Berwick shook his head. "I'm doing this for your sake, Wilde. He knocked you down. You were afraid he would kill you. A crowbar was on the ground. You rose with it in your hands. You struck him. It may very well be called self-defense." The smile became insidious. "Isn't that the way it happened, Wilde?"

"No. I gave you the facts half a dozen times. He was alive when I left."

Berwick clucked his tongue disapprovingly. "What alternative are you leaving us by your denial? You either murdered Doane in self-defense or you cold-bloodedly and deliberately murdered both Mrs. Doane and her husband."

I gawked at him.

"Exactly," he said, bouncing the pencil. "Two murders. Last night Mrs. Doane refused to leave her husband for you. You murdered her and drove off with her body and disposed of it somewhere."

"I said that's what Doane must have done."

"You said! You've told me a pack of lies. What do they get you? They convince me that last night you murdered Mrs. Doane and this morning you murdered her husband. You thought it would be easy to pin the murder on him after he was dead because he was already suspected of a two-year-old murder."

Wouldn't he ever stop bouncing that yellow pencil?

Berwick sighed. "Trying to be too smart in a murder is fatal. It becomes too complicated."

I tore my eyes from the pencil. I sank back in the chair and fumbled cigarettes out of my pocket. There were only two left.

"So there are the alternatives," he said. "We can forget about who murdered Mrs. Doane—he or you. You murdered Kenneth Doane, and that's enough to burn you. Unless you did it in self-defense."

He couldn't have had much if he was willing to settle on a self-defense plea, or maybe he considered that it would be an opening wedge to get me to change my story and keep talking and make mistakes until he had enough for first-degree murder.

I said: "Your tricks might work with the guilty person, but they can't work with me."

He bounced up to his feet. "I don't need tricks. Your fingerprints are on the crowbar. What do you say to that?"

"I say you're lying because I didn't touch the crowbar."

Berwick seemed to falter; his eyes lost confidence. He walked around the desk and jammed his fists into his pockets and snapped at the deputy: "All right, Ted."

I was taken back to the cell.

The meal that evening was no improvement over the first. I must have regained my taste for food because this time I more or less ignored it, except for the coffee. Then I took off my shoes and stretched out on the cot with the blanket under me. The mattress was not unendurably lumpy and so far no bugs had crawled out of it.

Daylight seeping in through the high barred window was fading. There was a naked overhead bulb, but the switch was outside. Anyway, I had no reason to want light.

Now and then I would remind myself that I should think through what had happened this morning, that somewhere there was something only I knew that could save me, but I couldn't keep my mind on it. My thoughts stopped and lingered on memories more vivid and real than murder or this cell: the second time I had laid eyes on Lela, when I had brought Maxine and she had come out on the porch, uncommunicative and almost hostile, and yet all of it starting at that moment, leading inexorably to those kisses days later in her kitchen and then, on a Sunday night, her coming to my bungalow and saying, "Undress me . . . but slowly . . . very slowly," and that had been the real beginning, because after that, after the intense and sometimes furious love-making, there had been no choice and no will but to go on and on.

As I lay in darkness in a prison cell, it seemed to me that last Wednesday night had been symbolic of it all, when I had groped through her dark house, as through a fog of fear and desire, to find her at last waiting for me soundless and expectant in a pink transparent nightgown. And last night— could it only have been last night?—I had lain in bed pretending to sleep while I had watched her remove her clothes by the fire, and we had not known that doom had caught up with us and was waiting outside in the person of her husband. But I had known an hour later and had gone after them and had spied on her dancing for him in a black veil—black like death—and eventually I had let her talk me into leaving her alone with a killer.

It was no good telling myself that I had done all I could. I had fumbled and blundered. Somehow I should have forced her to go away with me then and there, in only that scant wrapper if need be. What if he had gone after us with a rifle? I would have had her shotgun. I might have killed him then, as somebody else did later, but I would have been no worse off than I was now, and she would be alive. Or he might have killed us both, and I would still be no worse off.

The overhead bulb went on. A key turned in the door. I sat up. Conrad Hickey, carrying a small leather bag in one hand and a carton of cigarettes in the other, stepped into the cell. The door banged shut behind him.

His pleasant pixie face bore its usual cheerful expression. "Here are cigarettes, and Jessica packed a bag with your shaving things and a change of clothes. I left it with the desk sergeant."

"I'm especially grateful for the cigarettes." I started to open the carton. "You must expect me to be here quite a while," I said wryly.

"Not at all, not at all. We'll have you out shortly. Meanwhile you might as well keep yourself occupied. Jessica also packed in your bag your double-crostic book."

I wasn't a genius; I couldn't get anywhere with a double-crostic without my one-volume Columbia Encyclopedia and a dictionary and an atlas. But I didn't tell him that. About all I would care to do here would be to lie on my back and smoke.

Mr. Hickey sat on the chair and accepted a cigarette and we lit up. Then I said: "Has she been found yet?"

"I doubt if her body will be, at least not for some time. Bill tells me that last week Doane saw him and others looking for more of Alice's skeleton. Bill gave him a cock-and-bull story about a lost child, but it's likely that Doane suspected. He would have been more careful this time."

Dully I nodded. It must be a good theory because everybody was reaching it. I lay back on the cot and blew smoke at the ceiling.

"So far absolutely nothing has developed," he said. "No clues of any kind."

"What about fingerprints on the crowbar?"

"Impossible. That rough iron couldn't take an impression."

"Berwick told me my fingerprints were found on it."

Mr. Hickey leaned forward, anxiously. "Did you fall for it?"

"No. I had inside knowledge. I knew I'd never touched the crowbar."

Holding the cigarette pinched between his fingers, he

looked around.

"There are no ashtrays," I said. "I'll have to complain about the service."

He dropped the butt on the concrete floor and stepped on it. "I'm glad to see you keep up your spirit, Harry. You needn't worry. There's only a tenuous circumstantial case against you. As a lawyer with three times the experience of our bright young district attorney, I assure you that he hasn't enough for an indictment."

"Then what am I doing here?"

"Jim Berwick is hoping for some kind of break." Mr. Hickey scratched the corner of his mouth with his little finger. "I would have been here a good deal sooner, but there were ethical considerations. After all, my son Bill was one of the investigating officers. I could hardly defend a man whom it was his sworn duty to prove guilty. People would talk, and it wouldn't look right to his superiors. Bill and I discussed it and he agreed to ask to be removed from the case on the ground that he's your friend. His request was granted, and here I am with my legal talent, such as it is, at your disposal."

I said: "I don't want it."

"What? Are you saying you don't want a lawyer?"

"That's right."

Mr. Hickey rose and took three steps to a wall and turned and stopped at the foot of the cot. "Harry, did you do it?"

"Will you believe me if I deny it?"

He thought that over. "Frankly, I don't know. But I'd defend you anyway. I've never known a case with more extenuating circumstances. You naturally had reason to fear him as a killer after having found those bones. When you fought with him, you were justifiably afraid he'd murder you. You didn't intend to hit him that hard with the crowbar. You were terrified. At the worst, you had a mental lapse."

"No, thanks. I've only one defense, I didn't do it."

He resumed his seat. Under the naked bulb, his face looked strangely bloodless.

"You see the problem, Harry. If Doane murdered his wife, who but you killed him in reprisal?"

"His death was reprisal for which wife?" I said. "For Lela's murder or for Alice's murder?"

"Alice . . ." he muttered and looked up at the dark window. "I see. You don't trust me."

"No."

I closed my eyes against the glare of the overhead light.

Presently Mr. Hickey said: "Possibly it wasn't Doane who murdered Lela."

I tossed my cigarette to the floor and let it smolder there. "You want to be my lawyer, but now you think I killed both of them."

"My boy, I don't for a moment—" He looked shocked. "Is that what happened?"

"No. But what's the use of denying? I can give you more theories, but what's wrong with them is that they leave me out of it."

"It won't help you to be bitter."

"Why should I be bitter? Everything's wonderful."

He strode about the cell some more. Then he asked: "What are your theories?"

"There's one you won't care for—that Doane was murdered because somebody very much didn't approve of what he'd done to Alice. Another is that Doane didn't kill Lela and neither did I. Somebody else did because—"

I stopped.

Mr. Hickey finished it for me. "Because another man was in love with Lela Doane—perhaps, like you, he was her lover—and while he could take a husband, he couldn't take a competing lover and killed her in jealousy."

"Something like that."

"And then who killed Doane?"

"The same person because Doane knew who Lela's killer was."

Mr. Hickey sighed. "You can keep widening circles within circles until they take in practically everybody."

"That's right. Practically everybody."

He went to the door and watched me from there. "Harry, what can I do to make you take me into your confidence?"

"You're in my confidence already. You and about the whole world. I suppose it's in the newspapers."

"You're a prominent figure, you know. Reporters have come from as far as New York."

"I wonder if they'll put it on the sports page."

"I'm glad to hear you joke." Standing there against the door, he seemed to have withered physically. "Circles including almost anybody," he murmured. "Is that why you don't trust me?"

"Yes. Especially as I keep wondering why you were so anxious to drive me into Lela Doane's arms."

"Harry, that's a ridiculous notion."

"All right, everything's ridiculous," I said. "Love and death and me being here is ridiculous."

I lay back and closed my eyes.

I heard him rap on the door and I heard the deputy let him out. He said, "Good night, my boy," and I muttered, "Good night," and the door closed. The light went out. In darkness I fumbled for a cigarette.

Chapter Twenty-two »»»

IN THE MORNING Mrs. Hickey visited me, bearing a cardboard box not much less than half her size.

"A few things I threw together," she said and set the box down on the chair. "I've heard of the swill they serve here."

I untied the cord and raised the four flaps. The box contained a whole fried chicken, a home-baked apple pie, a shoebox full of home-baked chocolate cookies, half a salami, a couple of bags of potato chips, lots of candy, a dozen cans of beer.

"The prisoner's last meal," I said.

"Stuff and nonsense!" She dropped down on the cot and crossed her legs and shook a cigarette out of one of the packs her husband had brought me last night. "Harry, what's the matter with you?"

"What can be wrong? I have a roof over my head and a bed to sleep in and now the prospect of a couple of good meals."

Mrs. Hickey was not amused. Neither, for that matter, was I.

"Nobody tells me anything, not even my own son or husband," she complained. "Parts of poor Alice Barton's skeleton found and Bill and Conrad getting unreasonably scared when you disappeared for a few days and scandalous goings-on in the bungalow right under my nose, and most of it I have to find out from the newspapers." She paused. "So that was your mysterious visitor Sunday night! I must be getting slow-witted not to have guessed that it was bound to be a woman. The only difference between dogs and humans in heat is that dogs are open and honest. They shut up poor Maxine, but nobody shut up that—"

"Stop it!"

Mrs. Hickey uncrossed her legs and slouched back against the concrete wall. "I suppose at my age I ought to know better than to make moral judgments. Sex, they tell me, is a trap." She flicked ashes on the floor. "Poor Polly Wellman! She's pretty and in love with you and unmarried. But no, you had to go and get involved over your head with a . . ." She halted at that, as if she had finished the sentence.

I didn't say anything.

Through cigarette smoke she studied me. "You're a gentleman, Harry. You don't tell me to mind my own business. Because of my gray hair, no doubt." Her voice softened. "Did you love Mrs. Doane very much?"

"Yes."

"And now you don't care what happens to you. That's what I was driving at when I asked you what was the matter with you."

I closed the flaps of the box and placed the box on the floor and then didn't sit down on the chair. Standing, I said: "It's not that simple. I care and I don't care. At any rate, I'd like to get out of here."

"Then why don't you want a lawyer?"

"I see your husband has been talking to you."

"It was about time, wasn't it? He says you don't trust him."

She was a good woman, and I liked her. I didn't tell her what was on my mind. I said instead: "What's the good of having a lawyer who believes you're guilty?"

"What rot! You didn't do it. If you had, you would have said to anybody who would listen: 'Yes, I did it and I'm glad and I'd do it again because he murdered the woman I loved.' Like a defiant small boy. I don't say that would be wise, but that's the way men are, and you especially. Just before I told Jim Berwick—"

"Wait a minute. You spoke to the district attorney?"

"I should say I did. Just before I came down here, I stopped off at his office upstairs. Why, Jim's mother and I were friends before ever he was born. I told Jim: 'That poor boy is my nephew Dave's best basketball player and Dave sent him to North Set for me to take care of, and I intend to,' I said. I said: 'If you weren't still wet behind the ears you'd know that if he'd done it he would either admit it at once or he would have gone home and kept quiet about it.'"

"Bill thinks I tried to be smart."

"I know. That's what Jim Berwick told me too." She sniffed. "Of all the nonsense! I said to Jim: 'What was so smart about Harry killing a man and then bringing back a policeman to find the body?' I said: 'I can't think of anything more stupid, and with the marks of the fight all over him, and one thing you can say about Harry Wilde,' I said, 'he's far from stupid even if he is an athlete.' That's what I told Jim Berwick."

Maybe I wasn't smart, I thought, but somebody was smart.

Not too smart. Just smart enough.

Mrs. Hickey brushed loose gray hair from her brow. "If Jim has his way, he'll keep you here forever. You're very famous throughout the country. Without you it would be just another small-town murder. He's getting worlds of publicity through you, and what else does a politician want?" She lit a fresh cigarette. "I wish I could get in touch with Dave. The phone doesn't answer in his New York apartment."

"What can a basketball coach do for me in this spot?"

"He might talk you into sense. Conrad is really a very good lawyer."

I said nothing.

She stood up and pulled down her skirt and put a hand on my arm. "Would you want Conrad to send you another lawyer? He'll pick the best."

"And work with him behind the scenes, I suppose?"

Her lips drew together. "What have you got against Conrad?"

"Nothing."

She had to tilt her head way back to look up at me. With both of us standing, she didn't reach much above my chest.

"We'll get you out of here," she said crisply, "whether you like it or not."

"Oh, I'll like it all right."

She threw up her hands. "I give up trying to understand you."

I accompanied Mrs. Hickey to the door as if I were a host showing out a favored guest. I thanked her for the food. She said she hoped I would be free before it was necessary for her to bring a fresh supply and left. I heard the vigorous clicking of her heels in the corridor ahead of the deputy's shamble.

At lunchtime I spurned the prison food for the contents of Mrs. Hickey's box. A beer opener and a glass were included. The beer was tepid, but it tasted better than any I had ever had. I kept working on the beer, and between it and the cigarettes half the afternoon trickled by.

Then Gale swept into the cell.

She paused just inside the cell, hatless and with her blonde hair tight, tall and lithe and delightful to the eye in a pale-blue linen suit. Her hands clung to an immense straw handbag as she glanced distastefully about. The door banged behind her. Startled, she looked back at it.

"Hello, Gale," I said. "Sorry you don't approve of the accommodations. I don't either."

She roused. Saying, "You poor darling!" she came to me and kissed me chastely on the mouth and stepped back. "You sure got yourself into a mess," she said sympathetically.

"That's the word for it. Don't tell me you made the trip just to visit me?"

"Well, not directly," she admitted. "I read about it in the papers. It's in all the New York papers. There are pictures of you in your basketball outfit."

"I get it now. You came up for Maxine."

"Well, I couldn't leave Max in that place with nobody to take care of him, could I? I borrowed a car from Myron May this morning and drove out there, but nobody was there, not even Max. So I called the police and they told me that Max and those other dogs were taken by the Society for the Prevention of Cruelty to Animals. I'm on my way to pick him up, but I thought it only right to stop off to see you."

This was Wednesday. It was three weeks to the day and practically to the hour since she had brought Maxine to me. I had lived a life in those three weeks and I had died a kind of death.

I said: "Don't you know I'm supposed to have killed your boy friend?"

"The papers say you say you didn't do it."

"I didn't."

"Anyway, he wasn't my boyfriend."

"All right, merely a lover."

Gale's jaw jutted. "Hair-y—" she said angrily and suddenly lost her poise. She looked down at the chair and hesitated as if not sure that it wouldn't soil her skirt, then she sat on it with the straw handbag on her knees. "Nothing like that happened, really."

"Gale," I said, "you don't dislike me, do you?"

"Why, what a thing to ask! I don't love you anymore, of course, but, after what we've been to each other, I'm fond of you."

"All right then. I'm in a mess, as you pointed out. I need all the help I can get. Will you help me?"

"I don't see how I can."

"Probably you can't, but every bit of knowledge might help. What happened between you and Kenneth Doane when you drove him to New York Wednesday?"

She chewed the orange lipstick on her lower lip. "You don't seem to believe a word I say," she complained petulantly.

"I think you fell pretty hard for Doane."

"Well, he was terribly attractive."

"All right. And he attracted you all the way up to North Set."

"What if he did?"

"Look, Gale, I'm not concerned with your morals. My own weren't so hot. After all, his wife and I ... Well, you must have heard about that."

"I certainly did. And I can't imagine what you saw in her. She struck me as being cold and dowdy and not even pretty. I flatter myself, Hair-y, that once you had better taste."

She had to be worked carefully; I made myself dismiss Lela Doane with a shrug. "Well, nobody can deny that Kenneth Doane was about as handsome as they come. It was natural for you to fall for him."

"But—" Her face clouded. "Hair-y, will it really help if I tell you?"

"It might."

"Then I will. Kenneth Doane told me his name when you took me swimming that day I brought Max. I couldn't get him out of my mind. I looked up his number and called him one day from New York. He thought I called because of Max; that was how I found out he was boarding Max. You know what happened then; you were really clever, darling. But you're all wrong about what happened when we got to New York that night."

"How was I wrong?"

"It's not flattering to tell you this, but if it will help . . ." She lowered her eyes like a shy virgin. "He wouldn't even come up to my apartment for a drink. He said he didn't drink. I said we could have coffee and he said he wouldn't sleep if he drank coffee that late. And do you know, we stood there in front of my building arguing. I've never had to throw myself at a man, and I didn't really throw myself at him, but I just couldn't get him to come up." Her mouth curled. "That hick!"

"Don't tell me he didn't know the score?"

"Oh, he knew all right. That's why I said this story wasn't flattering. Darling, do I look all right to you?"

"You look delicious, but there are some men who are faithful to their wives."

"That's a laugh," she said. "All the time his wife was playing around with you. No wonder when he found out—"

She stopped. Murder was a sensitive subject; she didn't want to embarrass me.

"Do you know why he went to New York?" I asked.

"Some kind of meeting next day with other animal doctors. I wasn't interested." Gale's orange-tipped fingers tightened on the handbag. "Imagine me standing on the street and practically begging a man! And then he wanted to shake hands when he left. I turned my back to him and went into the house."

"A woman scorned," I muttered.

Her head lifted. "What did you say?"

"I appreciate your telling me this."

"But it doesn't help, does it?"

"I don't see how, but thanks anyway."

Gale stood up. "I still have to pick up Max and then there's that long drive." She arched against me when we kissed good-bye. "Darling, you know I wish you the best of luck."

"I know."

When she was gone I opened another can of beer.

Chapter Twenty-three »»»

LATER THAT AFTERNOON the district attorney sent for
me. I sensed a kind of desperation in Berwick's bounding
and prowling and jittering as he kept endlessly repeating
himself. After two hours of that I was returned to my cell,
where I finished everything in Mrs. Mickey's box except the
candy and four cans of beer.

At eight o'clock I made the final trip up those two flights
of stairs with the morose deputy. Berwick, alone in his office,
told me irritably that I could go home if I promised not to
leave North Set. That was a fair price. I promised and went
down to clean my belongings out of the cell. I gave the
deputy the remaining candy and beer and also five packs of
cigarettes. We shook hands.

In the street I found Bill Hickey waiting for me. He was
out of uniform and, instead of his police sedan, his convertible was at the curb.

"I heard you were being released," he explained, "and I
figured you could use a ride home."

"Thanks."

We drove through twilight.

"It was Pa who talked the D.A. into letting you go," Bill said. "You tried to brush Pa off, but he went to bat for you anyway."

"Should I get down on my knees and thank him?"

He threw me a sharp, sidelong glance. "Why don't you like the old man?"

"I do, but that's not the point," I said and let it go at that. So did Bill.

After a silence he said: "Pa told Jim Berwick to put up or shut up—to charge you or release you. Berwick was in a spot. It's strictly a circumstantial case; nothing more's been found to back it up. Even if he found air-tight evidence against you, the fact that you'd had a fist fight with Doane would be on your side. A smart lawyer like Pa could show that you had plenty of reason to be scared of Doane and to fight him: he'd killed his first wife and there was his second wife missing. And it's hard to prove that a killing in the midst of a bloody fight like that was premeditated. At the most manslaughter, but Pa wouldn't let the D.A. get away with that either. He'd put you on the stand and you'd say that in the middle of the fight Doane tried to sock you with the crowbar and you got it away from him and socked him instead. Open-and-shut self-defense, and under the circumstances the jury would believe you."

"Berwick needn't have worried," I said. "I'll never plead self-defense."

"Likely a straight not-guilty defense would also do it. There's no corroboration to the circumstantial case—no bloody clothes of yours or anything like that. And then you were the one who phoned the police and told me all about the fight and took me to the Doane place. Could be that was being smart—"

"Too smart, you said at the time."

"Yeah, but Ma, who's pretty shrewd about people, says—"

"I know. She says that if I were the killer, it wouldn't have been smart of me but stupid to take you there, and she doesn't think I'm stupid. It's the nicest compliment I ever got."

"Did you know she went up and fed Jim Berwick that line herself? What a woman Ma is! The thing is that jurors would have minds that run just like hers. Could be Ma impressed Berwick even more than Pa did. He's a new D.A. This would be his first big case and with lots of publicity. You're not any Joe Shmoe. I didn't realize how famous you are, Harry, till I saw all the fuss the papers made over you after your arrest. Berwick wouldn't crawl out on a limb with what he had and with all that limelight on him, and he couldn't keep on holding you while he waited for something to break."

"In other words, I'm still where I was yesterday morning—the chief and only suspect."

Bill hunched his broad shoulders over the wheel and said: "Berwick and the county police and the state police will be working and digging and ready to pull you in again at any moment. The only reason I can shoot off my mouth to you like this is I'm off the case."

"So I heard from your father."

Without taking his gaze off the road, he said: "Why don't you trust Pa? Because of me?"

"That could be it."

He nodded grimly. "I told you the other day that I'd get Doane in some way, but I meant finding enough legal evidence to convict him of Alice's murder."

"Did you think you could ever find such evidence?"

"I was going to try damn hard. You figured that if I'd killed Doane and Pa found out or even suspected, he'd cover for me by throwing you to the wolves. Well, you don't know him."

"Perhaps I don't."

"Anyway, how could I have done it?" Bill argued. "How long was it between the time you left Doane and the time I picked you up at your bungalow?"

"Less than fifteen minutes."

"And how come I happened to get there during just those fifteen minutes?"

"You were in the neighborhood. You picked me up at the bungalow a couple of minutes after I called police headquarters."

"My God," he said, "how far can coincidence go?"

"It went a long way in this case because Doane was murdered within that short period. Or maybe Doane wasn't the only one who watched my bungalow last night. Maybe somebody followed me to the Doane place and heard Lela tell me to come back next morning and whoever it was made certain plans. I'm even getting a notion that it wasn't necessarily Doane who killed Lela."

"All that complication doesn't make any more sense than all that coincidence."

I slumped lower in the seat. "I know. The only thing that makes sense is that I'm guilty, so that's what everybody believes."

"I wouldn't say that. Ma and Pa don't believe it."

"What about you?"

He shrugged. "I'm off the case and the hell with it."

"I don't suppose you're sorry he's dead."

As he drove, his body made a taut line from hip to shoulder. "I sure would've hated for him to get away with having murdered Alice."

There was no more to be said. We drove in silence.

When he stopped the car at his house, Bill asked me to come in for a drink with himself and his folks. I said I was still full of beer and walked across the lawn to my bungalow.

Nothing in the bungalow had changed since yesterday morning. The police who had searched it had tidily closed drawers and replaced furniture; the bed remained unmade and the breakfast dishes were on the table. But somehow everything was different. The bungalow was lonelier than the prison cell.

I built a fire and sat before it until the heat and the dancing flames put me to sleep. During the night I awoke and undressed and flopped into the empty bed.

Chapter Twenty-four »»»

FOUR WOMEN SAT sheltered from the late morning sun on the porch of Wellman's store. One of them was Mrs. Wellman. They stopped talking when I pulled up in my car and they gawked. They had been talking about me, of course— me and the Doanes and murder. No doubt in the last two days North Set must have given itself over wholly to enjoying the juiciest scandal it had ever had.

Mrs. Wellman didn't beam at me. I had ceased to be an eligible male for her marriageable daughter. On the contrary.

"Is George in?" I asked her.

She seemed to relax a bit, probably because I hadn't asked for Polly. "I think he's in the back yard."

The buzzing of excited conversation resumed as I rounded the corner of the building.

I walked along the side of the house to the fenced-in yard bordered by flashing colorful flowers. They were Polly's handiwork. In a hammock under the only tree in the yard, an ancient and gnarled oak, George Wellman lay reading what I guessed would be a racing form. His bare chest was skinny and pale and hairy.

"So they let you out," he said. "What'd you have—pull?"

"I had lack of guilt."

"Huh! That's not what I heard." George let the paper flutter to the grass; sure enough, it was a racing form. "So you're the pure Harry Wilde! Wouldn't do nothing they don't teach in Sunday school. Mind if I laugh?"

I pulled up a metal outdoor chair and sat down.

"Don't laugh too soon," I said. "They're looking for the killer."

"What's that to me?"

"The police might be interested in how Lela stopped you from blackmailing us when you barged in on us in her kitchen."

"Why'd they be interested?"

"It could be she had some hold over you and it was important to you to shut her up."

"Hey, wait a minute." He rolled on his side; the hammock swung. "She was knocked off by her husband or maybe by you. That's the way I heard it."

"Are you sure that's the way it was?" I said and stared at him, making myself smile.

George squirmed. "Say, Lela didn't have nothing on me."

"She told me she knew how to make you keep your mouth shut."

"Yeah. She was a clever babe. I'll tell you what she said. She said if I tried to pressure you or told her husband, she'd go to the law and swear she was a witness that I offered you a bribe. She said she didn't give a hoot for her husband any more and was nuts over you and was going to divorce him anyway and marry you, so it'd be no skin off her if she was a witness against me."

"You believed her?"

"You're darn tootin' I believed her. I knew Lela maybe better than anybody. A funny dame. Strictly one-man. Hell, if she let you spend the night with her, it meant she was nuts over you like she said and would do anything for you. Lela was no tramp."

Sunlight formed patchy patterns through the trees. I stared at one in the shape of a narrow triangle, and at the apex a daisy swayed.

"Tell me about Lela," I said.

"Such as what?"

"I only made love to her. I never got to know her."

George turned on his back. The hammock swung gently.

"A funny dame," he said. "Got to know her four-five years ago in the city. She was rooming with a dame I was doing some loving with, a blonde, name of Mary. Lela was going around with Brick O'Connell, a bookmaker. He was taller than you even and red-headed. Seems Lela preferred 'em tall. Like I said, she had an apartment with Mary, though many a night she didn't come home. Those nights she spent with Brick and nobody else. I know on account of me being there so much and Mary telling me everything and guys talking how they couldn't get to first base with her. There wasn't a guy didn't hanker for her. She wasn't the prettiest babe you ever saw, but she had something. I don't know. She was so quiet-like, even at a party. She didn't smile much or talk much and never raised hell, but. . ." He stroked his mustache. "What the hell, you should know what I mean."

"Yes," I said. "I know."

"Then she and Brick broke up. Mary told me she just got tired of him. Brick went off to the west coast and Lela spent all her nights home. Strictly a one-man woman. You know what she was doing to support herself? She worked in a department store. She stood all day on her feet selling ladies' undies or something when there was guys ready and willing to set her up in style, with mink coats and penthouses and everything. There was even guys loaded with dough wanting to marry her. Mary and the other dames figured she had rocks in the head. Yeah! I don't mean Lela didn't keep coming to parties and letting guys take her to nightclubs and shows, but it was strictly hands off. You can take my word. After me and Mary broke up, I spent plenty on Lela, taking her everywhere, but not even a good-night kiss."

George shook his head incredulously. "Strictly love with her and it had to be the right guy. Just three guys I know of in five years—Brick O'Connell, then Doane, then you. And not getting anything out of it. Like with that horse doctor she married. Giving up all the fun in New York, giving up clothes and jewels and all the things a dame wants, and burying herself in this hick town in a broken-down house and seeing almost nobody and going nowhere." He scowled at the overhead canopy of branches. "How do you figure a dame like that?"

Behind us a door opened and closed. I glanced around; there was nobody.

"I understand she met Kenneth Doane through you," I said.

"I guess I'm responsible. There was a dame, name of Agnes Hazard, used to be a friend of mine and stepped off a chorus line to marry a rich guy who made men's suits. They had a swanky place in Maine and she invited a crowd of old friends up for a few days. I was invited and Lela was too and I had a car in those days and said I'd drive her up. It was the middle of May, I remember. We had to stay somewhere overnight on the way, and sure I had ideas—anyway, hopes.

What I would've given for just one night! I made the mistake of stopping off here to see my folks because it was on the way." George sighed. "Why kid myself? She wouldn't have bunked with me that night, anyway. Maybe I wasn't tall enough. When my old lady suggested we stay here overnight, Lela said sure and that's the way it was. She slept with Polly and I slept in my old bed."

"How did she meet Doane?"

"That same evening. Lela and I were taking a walk. She said she was nuts about the country and never had a chance to walk in the moonlight. I figured maybe she'd get romantic." He laughed without mirth. "Fat chance. Anyway, we met Doc Doane walking along and we stopped and I introduced them. I'd met the guy the summer before when I spent time with the folks and he used to come into the store. That's all there was—a few words and we walked on. Then next morning, when I was putting our bags in the car, I saw them standing at his station wagon in front of the store. I guessed he'd come to buy something. I didn't think a thing about it. Ten minutes later we were on our way to Maine. She didn't say a word about him. She never had anything to say anyway."

"Did you see Lela and Doane together in New York?"

"Naw. Fact is I hardly ever saw her after that. Then I came up next spring to visit the folks and you could've knocked me over when Polly told me Lela was married to Doc Doane. I went over to see her, and there she was in that broken-down house with a bunch of dogs almost mobbing me and wearing something the cat must've dragged in—Lela, who could've had a guy with a million bucks if she'd wanted. How d'you figure a dame like that? I can't."

The shifting sun had plucked me out of the shade. I was

beginning to sweat, but I sat there simmering with my thoughts far away and on nothing definite—just sitting and thinking of her without form or substance, as if it would hurt too much to recall in detail her passionate body.

". . . your mail," George Wellman was saying. I had almost forgotten he was there.

"What?" I said.

"Seems you're getting company."

Polly Wellman, slender and tight in a simple striped cotton frock, was coming toward us over the grass. In her hand were letters and newspapers. That would be my mail; these days it was always accumulating at the post office.

She handed me the mail without looking directly at me. "I'd like to speak to you in private."

"Sure, Polly. What is it?"

"In private," she repeated.

Abruptly George sat up on the hammock. He frowned. He appeared about to say something, but he didn't. He bent over to pick up the racing form. Polly had started to walk toward the house. I moved after her.

Side by side and at the same time far apart we walked along the side of the house to the road. Her head was down. I took quite a while thinking of words. Then I said about the only thing I could have. "I'm sorry about all this, Polly."

She didn't answer, didn't look up. By then we had reached the front of the building. I was relieved to find that the women were no longer on the store porch.

"We can talk while we take a drive," I suggested.

She moved on to my parked car, but she didn't get in when I pulled the door open. She looked up at me with her blue eyes glistening wetly. I hoped desperately that she wouldn't burst into tears.

"What I have to say will take only a minute," she said. "I was the one who told Dr. Doane about you two."

I wasn't surprised. A woman's voice, Lela had said, and Polly was a woman who knew because her brother had told her.

"It doesn't make any difference now," I said.

"It does. How I hate myself! I phoned Dr. Doane and didn't give my name and said that his wife and you . . ." She averted her face and light-brown hair fell over her rounded cheek. "I thought he'd make her give you up and then you—then you—"

A sob shook her.

"Let's forget it, Polly," I said.

"How can I?" Her voice was back under control. "I was the cause of it all. If I hadn't told him, all this wouldn't have happened."

"It was bound to come out anyway."

She faced me then, and there was a kind of wild defiance in her face. "I had to do it. I loved you. I don't care what you did. I still love you."

She ran into the store.

I groped for a cigarette in my shirt pocket. I was shaken. I was remembering how Polly had said that evening when I had driven her home in the rain from the movies, "I'll kill her before I'll let her have you," and when I had scoffed and called it nonsense, she had said, "You think it's nonsense, do you?" and, like now, she had dashed into her house.

I had my light. As I drew smoke deep into my jittery insides, I found myself looking directly at Mr. and Mrs. Wellman. They were inside the store, watching me through the plate-glass window, and their eyes hated me.

I climbed into my car and drove away.

Chapter Twenty-five »»»

I DROVE UNTIL I was hungry and I ate in a roadside restaurant and went on. I had no destination; at random I chose side roads away from centers of population. I drove through fields and woods and over mountains, alone with my loneliness, and probably I wouldn't have returned to North Set if I hadn't promised Berwick and if my absence wouldn't have been misunderstood. Toward evening I ate again and headed back.

Mr. Hickey sat at his easel under the maple. He wasn't painting. He watched me get out of my car. I hesitated, then walked over to him.

The easel was blank, no paper or canvas on it. His paint box sat unopened on the ground. Gravely, without greeting, we looked at each other, and I had an idea he was trying to make up his mind.

"Do you want to tell me something?" I said.

He rubbed his nose with the flat of his hand. "You were right, Harry. I was anxious for you to fall for Mrs. Doane."

"Did you paint that nude of her purposely to show it to me?"

"No, I'd painted it months before you came here. For my own purpose." A flicker of his pixie smile appeared. "Her animal magnetism fascinated me. Not being young like you, and at any rate content to remain a respectably married man, I daydream with paints. I had no intention of showing anybody that picture. You're the only one beside myself who's seen it."

"I don't understand," I said.

Mr. Hickey plucked a dandelion from between his feet. "I was very fond of Alice Barton. I had hoped she and Bill would marry." His fingers mangled the dandelion's golden head. "Alice married Kenneth Doane. She broke Bill's heart. Two years later she disappeared and rumors started. At first I scoffed at them, but as time passed I changed my mind. Bill refused to investigate. The pride of a young man who had been jilted. He couldn't bear to take the chance that he would find out Alice had become a tramp, or at least that she was the kind who flitted from man to man."

"Why didn't you investigate on your own?"

"But I did. I learned that Alice and Doane hadn't been divorced in Florida and that that winter he and his second wife had been married in New York by the county clerk. But what did that prove? Probably he was guilty of bigamy, if nothing else, but, with Alice missing, not even such evidence could be obtained. I kept my mouth shut."

"Wait a minute," I said. "Did you offer to paint Mrs. Doane's portrait to give you an excuse to hang around their house?"

Wryly the corners of his mouth lifted. "That's a shrewd guess. Yes, I was playing detective. But during those hours I spent with her on her porch I didn't see or hear anything that helped." He glanced away from me. "When you had lunch with us that day after you met her and showed you were interested in her, I tried to play God."

"So that's it," I said slowly. "Your idea was that if I became her lover I'd do my damnedest to pin murder or at least bigamy on him so I could have her for myself."

"It was partly that, but a forlorn hope. Why would you have been able to do better than I?"

"I found those bones."

"Accident. Listen to me, Harry. Doane had messed up Bill's life by taking Alice away from him. Maybe someday Bill will marry, but he's no longer young. He has no wife and Jessica and I have no grandchildren. It's a bitter thing, Harry. I wanted Doane punished—for that and for whatever he had done to Alice. I wanted the woman he loved taken away from him as he had taken Alice away from Bill."

"And you used me and Lela for revenge," I said contemptuously.

"Revenge?" Mr. Hickey thought about the word. "Perhaps what I did hadn't even the dignity of revenge. I am afraid it was basically boredom, heaven help me. Like using paints to denude women. I'm not used to inactivity, and evidently my art is no complete substitute. It's a shameful thing to confess, but in the last two days I've made myself face it. I was pulling strings to make you two lovers."

"You didn't succeed," I said.

His eyes widened. "My dear boy, are you denying that you and Mrs. Doane—"

"No, but it was none of your doing. Don't flatter yourself into thinking that showing me that nude painting of her made me want her. It happened the minute I saw her. I would have wanted her if you had never existed."

"I suppose so," he muttered.

Bill pulled up to the house in his police car. He didn't come over. He waved to us and entered the house.

"You hated Doane from the day Alice returned to North Set married to him," I said. "But that was nothing to how you felt about him when Bill told you we'd found part of her skeleton."

Mr. Hickey nodded absently.

The sun was gone, though it was still light. A breeze chilled me through my thin shirt.

I said: "Did you know Doane well?"

"Not well."

"A gentle man, Mrs. Doane called him."

"Gentle!" Mr. Hickey snorted. "Aside from being a chronic wife-killer, did you find him gentle when you fought him?"

"I fought as savagely as he did and I knocked him out cold and I don't think I'm particularly vicious." I let a silence hold between us before I said very quietly: "Do we really know that he ever killed anybody?"

Mr. Hickey rose with his paint box. He looked at the sky and then at the stool and easel as if wondering whether to take them inside in case it rained. Then he looked at me.

"What are you getting at now, Harry?"

"I wish I knew."

That was true enough. I didn't know anything. I went back to my bungalow.

I didn't go in. I kept walking to the road and then up the road the way that afternoon I had driven aimlessly in my car. But this time I had a destination, though I didn't know why I wanted to go there.

I reached the Doane house in twilight. No snarling, lunging dogs would ever again run out from there to meet a visitor. There was a hollowness in the silence of the place, as if it existed in a vacuum.

The porch steps creaked under my feet. Even that brought back memories, how they had creaked when I had gone into that house for our first and only complete night together. The door was locked; the police must have shut down the house. But why did I want to go in there?

I tried the barn door. It slid open. Little light was left. I saw broken stalls, a rusted harrow, discarded oil drums, a couple of wrecked tires—a storehouse for junk and a home for dogs. Only the junk was left.

What did I expect to find? The police had gone over everything.

The paddock gate was wide open. For a long moment I stood staring at the gate as if trying to discover something about it. I shook myself and stepped into the paddock.

The quarter of the dead horse was there—what the dogs had left of it. Doane had died before he'd had a chance to take it in from the sun and the police hadn't bothered. The smell of it clogged my nostrils and twisted my stomach.

Suddenly I wanted no part of that place or anything that had ever been there. There had been too much flesh and desire, and now all that was left was decay and corruption.

In darkness I walked home.

I piled all the remaining kindling and logs in the wood-bin into the fireplace. These nights a fire was my one companion. Without it I didn't think I could endure the emptiness of the bungalow in the evening.

I wondered if I was going to pieces.

The fire was a comfort. Sitting close to it, I could relax a little. My insides relaxed with the drowsiness it produced; my thoughts blurred; and that was the best thing that could happen to them. Like getting drunk and dulling memory.

The opening door roused me. It was at my back. I hadn't the energy to stir. "Who's there?" I mumbled.

There was no answer. The door closed. I heard slow footsteps approach on the bare floor. I turned my head then. She was in the room.

She had stopped moving. There was no light but fire-light, and in its dim fringe she was taller than I remembered, slimmer, and her face was somehow more vivid. She was changing in my dreams of her, even in my waking dreams.

I sank lower into the chair and stared into the fire. I was afraid. The illusion had been too real.

"Darling, don't you want me any more?" she said.

Now her voice! The sound of it frightened me. When you started hearing the voices of the dead, it was a sign that your mind was crumbling.

I turned my head and she was still there. I looked into her dark eyes and then I knew.

"Lela!" I cried, stumbling up to my feet.

She came into my arms, vibrant and passionate and alive.

Chapter Twenty-six »»»

AFTER A WHILE I stepped back to let my eyes absorb her. I felt that I had been reborn.

"You look different," I said.

"That's because you've never seen me dressed up." Lela made a complete turn, like a fashion model. "Do you like me this way, honey?"

I wasn't sure. She was no longer the simply and even dowdily dressed woman living in an isolated crumbling house in the country where style didn't matter. She wore a beige shantung-silk dress with buttons running down in front from the high collar to the hem, and over it a tiny jacket of the same color and material. On her black hair sat a white, small-brimmed panama hat. Her high-heeled shoes made her taller; for some reason she also appeared slimmer. Her mouth was redder, fuller with paint, more sensuous, and whatever she had done to her dark eyes made them more vivid.

She had become too much like any other smartly dressed woman. In a way, she was a stranger.

She removed her tiny jacket and her hat and placed them on the table where her black plastic handbag already lay. Her hairdo, like the rest of her, had become sleek and fashionable and sophisticated. And her smile was different too, the way she stood smiling with her eyes as well as her mouth, nothing aloof or enigmatic, complete and generous, giving all of herself.

I reached for her then and she put her hands on me fiercely and rose on her toes.

"It was awful being away from you, Harry," she said against my mouth. "I love you so."

Lela had said it. She had called me darling and honey and Harry, and she had said she loved me.

I said: "Where were you?"

The question brought us both back to the immediate past. Without moving, she seemed to go away from me.

"I read in the paper about what happened to—to Kenneth," she said.

"Everybody thought you were dead. We believed he'd killed you."

"I read that too." Her arms dropped from me. Suddenly her painted face looked garish and in some subtle way unfamiliar in the uncertain firelight. She said, "Harry, did you . . .?" and looked away from me.

"No," I said.

"The papers said you had a fight. If you did it by accident . . ."

"I didn't," I said harshly. "You can believe me."

Lela swung around to me and clung to me with her face against my shoulder. "I believe you," she said brokenly and I felt her shiver.

"Did he mean so much to you?"

"No. I had stopped caring for him. But I didn't want him hurt."

I pulled her down with me to the wing chair. She kicked

off her shoes and curled up on my lap and snuggled into me.

"Now tell me where you were," I said again.

"I went to New York," she said in a low monotone. "I thought I could handle Kenneth. I could have if I'd gone to bed with him. But I couldn't let him touch me. Not after you. He acted crazy. I had never seen his eyes like that. He said if I slept with you I could sleep with my husband, and he held my arm and hurt me. I made myself kiss him and be affectionate and I said I'd be right back from the bathroom. I went out to the hall and slipped downstairs. In the hall closet there was an old dress and a pair of old sneakers. I put them on."

"Oh, is that why I found your wrapper in the kitchen?"

"Yes, I dressed in the kitchen. All I had was the cotton dress and the sneakers. My other clothes were upstairs in the bedroom where he was waiting for me. My bag with money in it was up there too. I had to leave just the way I was. I didn't even take time to look for a flashlight. I made my way to the highway and waited there till daylight. The driver of one of those huge hauling trucks gave me a lift. He was going to New York. He was very nice. He bought me lunch and when he dropped me off in New York he wanted to lend me a few dollars, but I took only a dime for the subway."

"Why didn't you come to my bungalow?"

"Don't you see how dangerous that would have been? I was afraid that as soon as Kenneth missed me he would go there with the rifle."

"He didn't."

"I didn't dare take the chance. The crazy way he was feeling there was no telling what he'd do." Her mouth trailed over the side of my neck. "I planned to get in touch with you and have you join me in New York."

"Why didn't you?"

"But honey, this is only Thursday and I didn't reach New York till Tuesday afternoon. I went to a girlfriend's apartment. I hadn't slept the night before and so much had happened and I was dead on my feet. She gave me a hot bath and put me to bed. All next day I stayed in the apartment resting."

"Didn't you see a newspaper?"

"My friend is a sweet girl but not very bright and she never buys a newspaper. The first time I left her apartment was this morning when I went shopping. She lent me money and enough of her clothes to get me decently to the stores. I bought every single thing I'm wearing now and had lunch and went to a beauty parlor. I read a paper while I was sitting under a dryer, and that was how I found out. I almost fainted right there on the chair."

"You poor kid." I stroked her leg that was smooth and warm under nylon.

"All I could think of was that I had to rush to you, and you were so far away. It was maddening, all that waiting— waiting for them to finish with me in the beauty parlor, waiting almost two hours in Grand Central for a train, then the train going so slow." She held me tight. "But now I'm here, darling, and everything is all right."

Past her sleek hairdo, I saw that the fire was beginning to die. I thought of replenishing it and then remembered that the woodbin was empty.

"We have to let the police know you're alive," I told her.

"Does that mean either we'll have to go to them or they'll come here?"

"Yes."

"Must we tonight, our first night when we don't have to pull down shades and lock doors?" Lela took my face between her hands. "Honey, can't it wait till tomorrow?"

Her mouth moved up to mine, avid and demanding. I felt all of her demanding me. Why not tomorrow? My hands going to her was my answer.

She slipped off my lap. Shorter again without shoes, she stood on the hearth and stretched her arms languidly.

"Do you remember the first time I was here and you undressed me?" she said softly.

I rose and she stood motionless as I opened dress buttons. Slowly, she had said that first time, and it was even slower now because there were many buttons from the high collar to the hem, and my fingers were clumsy, fumbling, my hands shaking. I was kneeling at her feet when I had the last button open. I straightened and when the beige dress was off her I saw that it was a girdle that made her look slimmer.

Her hands were clenched at her sides. She seemed to be holding herself together, taut like a wire stretched almost to the breaking point and at the same time so soft and ripe and warm, and my hands kept shaking. Slowly . . . so much more slowly than the first time, garters to be unfastened, full-length hose to be peeled off and the complications of a girdle. When I stood, my knees were like water.

"No, don't touch me yet," she said softly. "Bring a blanket."

This too would be like the first evening together, on a blanket in front of the fire—always a ritual, always an interlude to prepare for ecstasy. I pulled the blanket off the bed.

She stood away from the fireplace, her face in almost complete shadow and the glow on the rich golden-tan curves of her. This was as I had known her, without the unfamiliarity of fancy clothes, still and curiously remote in her nakedness, the searing, blending, maddening beginning delayed in almost unendurable tension. I felt her watch me as I spread the blanket.

The phone rang—a jarring, violent sound outraging our privacy. I moved to the phone.

"Do you have to answer it?" she said.

I turned. She was sitting on her legs on the blanket. Her hands moved up to her hair to take it down and her breasts lifted and I couldn't stop looking at her.

She didn't, after all, do anything about her hair. She stretched out on the blanket, her toes arched toward the languishing fire.

"You're still dressed," she said. "Don't torment me. Come on!"

The phone kept ringing. It might go on for some time and then whoever it was might shortly try again. I wanted no intrusion tonight in this snug and passionate world we were making for ourselves here in the bungalow.

"It'll take only a minute," I told her and picked up the phone.

Gale's voice said: "Is that you Hair-y? I read in the paper that they released you. I'm so glad."

"Where are you, Gale?"

"I'm home. This is the third time I tried to get you since this afternoon, but there was no answer. Hair-y, do you know that woman, that Mrs. Doane everybody thinks was killed, is alive after all?"

I just stood there.

"Hair-y, did you hear what I said? Mrs. Doane is alive. I saw her in New York this afternoon. Are you listening?"

"Where did you see her?" I said.

"I was crossing Fifth Avenue at Thirty-ninth Street. She was walking on the sidewalk. I thought it couldn't be Mrs. Doane because she was supposed to be dead, and she was dressed so different, I mean rather smartly. But I went up to her and I said, 'Mrs. Doane,' and she stopped and looked at me. It was Mrs. Doane all right; I'd know her face anywhere. And do you know what she did? She didn't say a word. She just hurried off into the crowd."

I looked at Lela. She lay flat on her back, so still that she might have been asleep.

"Hair-y, are you there?"

"Yes," I said. "Did she recognize you?"

"Why, of course she did. We stood so close we could have touched each other, and we looked each other full in the face. Hair-y, I don't think she wanted to be seen."

There was no blood in my hand holding the phone. "No, she didn't want to be seen."

"I didn't know what to do. After all, the police think she's dead. Hair-y, what should I do?"

"I'll take care of it."

"Your voice sounds so queer. I suppose it's a shock. The police should be told, shouldn't they?"

"I'll take care of it, Gale. Good-bye." I hung up. For a moment I stood with my back to Lela, listening to the silence, then tiredly I turned.

Her cheek was against the blanket and her eyes were dark and expressionless watching me. She seemed to be holding herself in suspension.

"You murdered them," I said tonelessly.

Chapter Twenty-seven »»»

LELA SAT UP. She crossed her arms over her breasts as if in sudden modesty. Her painted lips parted and stayed that way without anything coming past them.

"It should have been clear as soon as I saw you alive," I said, "but I was stunned and happy and wanted you. Gale's call woke me up. You know what she told me."

The red lips moved. "We saw each other in New York. I forgot to tell you. What of it?"

"Everything," I said. "You ran from her. You were in panic because her seeing you messed up your scheme. Then you realized that you had to come here tonight to see what would happen when Gale told me that you were alive."

"What are you talking about?"

"I should have guessed when I saw the dogs out of their yard. Who else would they have let murder their master?"

The fire was gone except for smoldering ashes and the glowing back-log, but what light there was picked her out, concentrated exotically on her. It didn't matter. She might have been fully clothed instead of naked. All I felt was a cold lump in the pit of my stomach.

"You're talking nonsense," she said, crouching on the blanket.

"No. Everything I'd thought up to now was nonsense. Bill Hickey said it would have been too complicated and too much coincidence if anybody but I had killed Kenneth Doane. But that was when you were supposed to be dead. With you alive, there's no complication and no coincidence. It makes everything that happened simple and logical and connected."

Lela stood up. Her hands moved over her stomach and to her hips. The fire flared briefly, as if she had willed it to reveal her in all her womanliness.

"Have I changed?" she said huskily. "Am I any different from the woman you want?"

"You've changed. You're a murderer." I held onto a wing of the chair. "I suppose now you're going to dance for me. There's no black veil for you here. Anyway, it won't work with me. I think I have more will power than Kenneth Doane."

She kept looking at me, though I stood away from what remained of the fire and she couldn't see me as more than a blurred shadow. She touched her breast, then her face, then her hand fell limply and her shoulders drooped.

"Get dressed," I said. "I wouldn't like the police to find you here like this."

She stepped off the blanket and swung toward me, her hands seizing me, and thrust herself hard against me.

"Why must we lose each other? We'll be together always from now on." Her hips stirred against me. "That's what we both wanted all along, wasn't it? We have each other."

I remained rigid, feeling nothing for her.

"Making love to you," I said, "would be like making love to death."

"Don't say that. I didn't want to hurt Kenneth. Oh, my darling, kiss me."

She was on her bare toes, climbing up against me, trying to get her mouth to mine. I wondered how within a minute a man could have been so washed clean of desire for her. The demanding contact of her flesh infuriated me. I gripped her bare shoulders and flung her away.

She fell against the edge of the wing chair and sprawled from it onto the blanket. She lay face down, shuddering but voiceless, and I saw a bruise on her hip. I was sorry I had done that.

After a long moment she rolled over on her back. That brought her head to the flagstone hearth, and she lay there motionless and lax with her angular face static and her eyes empty.

I gathered up her clothes. I tossed them beside her and said: "Get dressed."

She pushed herself up to her knees and with slow, mechanical motions selected her undergarments and straightened up. But she didn't quite admit defeat. As she walked by me into greater dimness, her hips undulated provocatively. I wasn't provoked.

The floor lamp went on and I saw her step into her girdle. She could as easily have dressed without having put on the light. She was dressing before me, and taking her time at it, in a last attempt to make me succumb to her flesh before covering it. She couldn't understand. Watching her wriggle into her girdle had become indecent, even obscene.

I moved to the table and lit a cigarette.

"It's so unnecessary," she said. "Why must you do this to us?"

She was standing with the brassiere in her hand. Her

mouth, her eyes, the thrust of her body pleaded with me.

I said nothing. I walked stiffly to the phone at the other end of the bungalow.

"Harry, you're going to make yourself look foolish. What can you tell them?"

I turned. "All of it, beginning with the night George Wellman introduced you to Kenneth Doane."

"You don't know."

"I know now. It's become simple, uncomplicated. It all flows out of the kind of woman you are. There's only one thing that means anything to you, and that's the man you happen to want at the time."

"I want you."

"For how long, before you decide you'll have to get rid of me too?"

Lela went back to the fireplace, barefooted in her underwear. She sat on the edge of the armchair and drew on a stocking.

"If I did anything, it was for you," she said as she fastened a garter. "Because I loved you."

I started to laugh derisively and broke it off. There was truth in what she had said, though not by any means the whole truth. There was no rush to pick up the phone; the night was ahead and endless days. There was time to get it out into the open and look at it.

"You kept insisting that Kenneth Doane was kind and gentle," I said. "You should have known. Also faithful. Faithful to his wife—to his first wife and then his second wife. Gale told me she couldn't get anywhere with him, couldn't even lure him up to her apartment. You must have tried when he was married to Alice, and I think you failed too. You fell for that magnificent hulk of his with everything you had. George Wellman told me about you. A one-man woman. You passed up what few other women would, money and a fine home and fancy clothes, because the right man didn't go with them. When the right man came along it was the works."

Bending over to pick up her dress, she looked at me over a bare shoulder. "Is that supposed to be bad?"

"No, but murder is. That spring you must have come up here to see Doane. Most of the day Alice was away teaching school; you had plenty of opportunity to be alone with him. The house is so isolated that you could avoid being seen coming and going and being there with him. But Doane wouldn't play. No doubt he cared quite a lot for you. What happened afterward shows that he did. But he cared for Alice too, and in his dull, stubborn way he insisted on being faithful to her. Alice was in your way. And you murdered her."

She had been buttoning the dress from the bottom up. Her fingers froze on the third or fourth button from the top.

"Kenneth killed her," she said.

"Why? There were safer ways to get rid of her so he could marry you, and without shedding blood. She hadn't money for him to want to get his hands on, or not enough to count. Anyway, neither of you cared enough for money. Why not simply a divorce? Or if she kicked up a fuss over a divorce, why not go off together? Anything was easier and safer than murder." I shook my head. "Bill Hickey pointed that out, but finding the bones, the evidence, appeared to justify the rumors. Our minds became clouded. At the time enough hadn't happened to make me see clearly, and I hadn't yet found out what made you tick."

Lela put on her shoes. She sat down at the table and pushed

aside her jacket and hat and took a compact out of her handbag. The remoteness had returned to her face. She was the way she had been at the beginning of every meeting with me except tonight—restrained and indrawn and waiting.

"So it was you and you alone," I went on. "I think you did it when you learned he'd be away from home for a day or two or longer. You killed her. Did you use a crowbar or a hammer or did you strangle her or shoot her?"

Her profile was static as she dabbed powder on her strained, angular cheek.

"You killed her and buried her," I said. "Where we found her grave is another thing that shows he didn't do it. He knew the place; he'd have picked a better spot and dug deep. You're a strong woman, Lela, but only a woman, and you couldn't drag or carry her far. You dug at the foot of the knoll. You couldn't get down deep because of the ledge rock, but by then you were exhausted and panicky and that grave had to do. And then what? What did you tell him when he returned?"

She put up her compact. She looked at me with vacant eyes.

"She had a typewriter," Lela said, and her voice had again become dull and colorless. "I left a note with her name on it and took all her things away."

I dropped down on the bed, slumping there.

"You admit it," I murmured.

Her hand dipped into her handbag and came out with a gun. She turned in her chair to face me. It was a small, compact blue automatic, and it was very steady in her hand.

I said: "You came to kill me, but first you thought you might as well get in some love-making."

"No. I didn't want to use the gun."

"The way you didn't want to kill Doane?"

"Yes. But then I had to."

"And you have to kill me now because you know I've figured it out. You weren't sure. You said I didn't know. I told you too much."

She said nothing. She sat as if a carved part of the chair, and the gun was part of her.

I had to keep talking. She would want to hear the rest of what I had to say. She would delay that long. I forced speech past my throat.

"You left a note for Doane to find when he returned home. No doubt it said that she'd walked out on him for another man. And all her things were gone. He believed it. Murder wouldn't occur to him. He told nobody she had left him. She had no relatives and he was a taciturn man. School was out and nobody missed her. I suppose you waited a decent interval before you went to him. And he accepted you. There was no longer any reason not to. But sooner or later he found out. He must have come upon some of the bones."

With immense weariness she nodded. "The dogs brought them."

"Was that before or after he left North Set and didn't return for months?"

"Before. I wasn't living with him then. He didn't want me to—not openly. He thought he was still married to her and there would be a scandal. I went there now and then overnight and sometimes he came to my place in New York. Then one day he phoned me and told me."

"He wasn't sure that you'd killed her or even that it was Alice. He had to speak to you before he did anything."

"Yes."

"And you went to him and danced for him naked," I said. "I watched that the other night. I can understand how it was. He sitting there watching you, hypnotized, not able to see anything else or think of anything else. And then the love-making, probably right there on the floor, and he was help-less. Alice was dead and you were alive, so why not take what there was, especially since it was you? Your body gets a man. It got me for a while."

The gun dipped. "I love you, Harry. We can have such good times together."

I didn't want to talk about love, of her and me. The murders she had done kept my mind off it.

"He covered up for you," I said. "I guess he gathered up what the animals had left of his wife."

"Yes."

"He dug a new grave for her. Deeper this time. But there were parts of her he couldn't find. She'd been devoured and torn apart and scattered, and animals had made off with some of the bones. There was soft earth where that grave had been, a good place for animals to dig in, and some brought back bones they had taken elsewhere and buried them there."

She looked down at the little gun. I tensed, thinking that she would shoot then. But she did nothing at all; she seemed hardly to be breathing.

I said: "Then Doane drove off in his station wagon with the dogs. He couldn't have kept them with him during all those months; he must have boarded them somewhere. Then he stayed with you in New York."

"We went to Florida."

"All right, he drove on to Florida, as he had said he did, but not with Alice. With you. When enough time passed so a divorce could have been granted, you and he returned to New York and were married. Mr. Hickey said he considered the idea that Doane had committed bigamy. But that marriage was strictly legal, if nothing else was. His first wife was dead. You lived for a few months in New York and in the spring came back to North Set, where there was a house to live in and he had a profession that produced an income of sorts. You had what you'd done so much to get, that beautiful hunk of man to go to bed with every night. Then you . . ."

I hated to say it.

"Then I met you and fell in love with you," she said above the gun pointed at my heart.

I felt my mouth bitter. "Your desires are easily changed."

"I had stopped caring for him. I began to find him dull."

"And you looked for excitement with any man who came along."

"You weren't any man. I love you."

"Love?" I echoed and laughed harshly and briefly. "I don't know any more what love is. Do you?"

"It's what we did together and what we can keep on doing. I would have gone off with you right away. But I couldn't."

"You couldn't because of his hold on you. Not sex by that time; I believe that. He had an even stronger hold on you. He knew you'd murdered Alice, and the only way you could keep him quiet was by continuing his need for your body."

"I tried not to care for you. I knew it would only lead to trouble." She seemed somehow to be sitting lower in the chair, though her torso was erect. "I couldn't help myself. I thought once or twice with you would get you out of my blood, but always I wanted you more."

I sat slouched on the bed, thinking that that was why

until tonight she had had no words of endearment for me, why in all but the actual physical acts she had been aloof and restrained. She had wanted it to be transitory, to end soon if possible, without commitment and without my expecting more. But it hadn't worked out that way, for either of us.

She was the one to end the silence. "Then I realized that I had to have you all the time. I told you that the last time I was here. Don't you remember how I said I'd leave him and go with you?"

"I also remember that you said you needed time to work it out. I didn't know that you meant time to break his hold over you, time to get rid of him. You must have been planning then how to murder him and get away with it."

"No!"

"Maybe not," I conceded. "Maybe not till an hour later when he saw you come out of this bungalow and drove you home. And maybe not even then, because, if he could overlook murder, he could overlook a lover if you continued to dance for him and sleep with him and stay with him. He was trapped by you as much as you were by him. He was trapped by your body, and I can understand that. It's the one thing I'm in a position to understand easier than anything else."

"Harry!" Her red lips were parted. "Harry, you do care for me."

I didn't know. Tomorrow it might be different. Tomorrow my blood might flow again through my veins, but tonight I was safe from her. Perhaps it was shock. I wasn't able to care much about anything, not even very much if she shot me.

I said: "Bill Hickey warned me not to say anything about the bones, but that night outside your house I told you. I thought that would make you fear him enough not to go back in there with him. Fear him! That's a laugh. He was the one who needed protection. You realized you couldn't delay. If the police questioned him about the bones and really piled on him, there was too much risk he'd talk now that he knew you had a lover. You must have planned it all as we stood on the road. It was no longer a question of eliminating him so you could be with me. It was a question of saving your own neck. The police would suspect you at once, or you and me both. It would be a common pattern: a wife and her lover eliminating a husband. You decided to sacrifice me, make me the fall guy." My mouth twisted. "That's how much you loved me."

"I was frantic."

"Sure you were frantic. You were frantic for Doane; so you murdered Alice. You were frantic for your own safety; so you set the scene to murder him and have me take the rap. Before I left you that night, you had it all worked out. You told me to come for you in the morning, but you knew you wouldn't be there. Anyway, not in sight. By the way, you did go to bed with him after I left, didn't you?"

"I had to."

"Well, why not?" I said. "What did it mean to you, one more time with the man you knew you would soon kill? And when he'd had you and slept, you slipped out. You left every-thing of yours but what you had to wear so it would look as if he'd killed you the way he was supposed to have killed Alice. You waited hidden nearby for me to show up in the morning. You knew I'd go for the police when I found you weren't there. The fight was a little extra; both of us helped your scheme along there. When I drove off, you came out of hiding. You stood there talking to him till you saw a chance to pick up that crowbar and let him have it. I noticed your strong arms. I admired them. Strong and soft. Soft for love-making. Strong to smash a man's skull in."

I paused for her reaction. There was none. She was not a woman who would break at the memory of a murder or two. She sat silently with the gun pointing at me.

"The dogs were out of the paddock," I said. "That should have told me. They had become used to me, but they tried to get at me when I fought with their master. They would have torn to pieces whoever killed him. Except their mistress. You were the one person they wouldn't have touched."

"Are you finished?" she said with the beginning of impatience.

"Almost. You told me yourself how you reached New York, by getting a hitch on a truck. In New York, you had a friend you could trust, who would put you up and give you money. A woman friend, you said, but perhaps a man."

"A woman."

"All right. Your idea was to stay under cover and let the police assume you were dead, because then the finger of suspicion would never point to you. You could go to another part of the country, take another name—at any rate, sit tight till I was convicted of the murder and then you'd have little to fear. But you had no clothes; you had to go shopping. Gale saw you. That messed it up. You had to know how great your danger was if it became known that you were alive after all. I was the boy who could tell you. You'd read in the paper I'd been released. We'd make love and as I lay in your arms in front of the fire I'd spill everything I knew."

"I wanted you."

"You always took your hair down, but not this time. You didn't intend to stay long. And you brought a gun."

Abruptly she rose. Here it comes, I thought.

Quickly I said: "What good will killing me do?"

"The police won't figure it out the way you did. Nobody knows I'm here. I got a lift on a truck. The driver lives in Ohio; he'll be back there in two days. He'll be too far away to hear of me."

"What would you do without truck drivers?"

"The police won't suspect me because they won't know I'm alive. I'll disappear."

"Gale will tell them she saw you."

"It was in New York, not here, and I don't think she can be sure. And it's not evidence, just seeing somebody for a moment in a crowd." Her voice was as wooden as her face. "I don't think there's real evidence. All you said were words."

"Then why shoot me?"

"It'll be bad for me. I'll be in jail and maybe there'll be a trial. There could be other things, what they call clues. Why should I take the chance?"

"Not even for the man you claim you love?" I sneered.

"I've lost you anyway. You said so yourself." She touched the gun barrel with her other hand and complained angrily: "You're making me do it."

I stood up slowly, careful to make no movement that would startle her. All the same, the bed creaked. The gun jerked and my heart skipped a beat.

She started to shiver. All her body quaked and the gun shook. Something was happening to her, something deep inside her.

"Lela," I said, moving toward her gradually, "maybe it's not too late after all. I have an offer to coach basketball in South America. You and me together, Lela."

She looked at me. She stopped shivering. Step by step I was cutting the distance between us, getting closer to the gun.

"You're lying," she said thinly when I was halfway to her. "You're trying to trick me."

The muzzle focused on my chest, not steady now, but steady enough.

I moved on, watching her eyes, and I saw them die. I saw her face fall apart.

"I can't!" she whimpered.

I was close enough then to hurl myself at her with a chance to get the gun away from her. But I didn't. I stood watching her crumple—not physically but in the spirit. She slumped down on the chair, and the gun was out of her hand, on top of the tiny beige jacket beside her hat, and she put her hands to her face. Perhaps she wept, but I could not hear her.

I picked up the gun and stuck it into my hip pocket and went to the phone. That journey across the room was the longest I had ever taken.

My voice didn't act right when I gave the operator the number. For a small eternity the bell rang before Mrs. Hickey's voice came on.

"Is Bill in?"

"He's gone to bed. Who's this?"

"Harry Wilde."

"Oh, Harry. I didn't recognize your voice. I think Bill's asleep."

"It's important."

"Can't you tell me?"

"No."

The silence returned. I could hear my heart beat. I looked around. Lela sat without motion. I had become used to the stillness of her, but now it was stillness like death.

"Hello, Harry," Bill said.

"Come right over."

"What's up?"

"The mur—" I took a breath. "The person who killed them is in my bungalow."

I hung up. Through the side window I saw more lights go on in the Hickey house.

Lela said wistfully: "We could have had such fine times together."

She was smiling sadly, and that smile hurt more than anything else she could have done. More, in a way, than if she had shot me.

I felt as if I had betrayed her and myself too. But I'd had no choice, had I? What else could I have done?

It took Bill Hickey only seconds to arrive. He entered without knocking. He wore a pair of pants over his pajamas.

He stopped in the doorway and stared at her. It was very quiet in the bungalow.

His shoes squeaked as he stepped toward her. "Did you kill them, Mrs. Doane?"

"Yes," Lela said apathetically.

Chapter Twenty-eight »»»

AFTERNOON SUNLIGHT splashed through the windows and through the open door as I packed my books into a couple of boxes. Mr. Hickey appeared in the doorway.

"We're sorry you're leaving," he said.

It wouldn't have been polite for me to reply that I wasn't sorry. I merely nodded.

"Are you going back to New York, Harry?"

"Not for another five or six weeks," I said. "A teammate of mine, Luke McLarin, is director of a boys' camp in the Adirondacks, and he wants me to teach the kids basketball. There's only one woman in the place, the camp mother, and she's at least sixty. And I understand that no dogs are allowed."

"I can't blame you for being bitter."

There was nothing to say to that. I started to put books into the second box.

"There would never have been a conclusive case against Mrs. Doane," he said. "Any competent lawyer could have shown a reasonable doubt of guilt if she'd kept her mouth shut. Bill says she was more or less aware of that. Yet she confessed."

"Uh-huh."

"Bill says she brought a gun last night and admits she came here to kill you if she found you knew too much. Instead, she ended up by confessing." Gravely he contemplated me kneeling at the bookshelves. "She must have cared a great deal for you."

I wished he would let me alone.

"When I painted her portrait, I was acutely conscious of the turbulent emotions inside that quiet and controlled shell of hers," he said. "I mentioned as much to you in a rather dramatic way. She was capable of anything—violent lust and violent murder. I think she burned out last night when she was here with you. You extinguished the flame in her because she cared so much for you, and she no longer gives a damn what happens to her."

"Can't we stop talking about her?" I burst out.

Mr. Hickey nodded slowly and glanced through the door. Then he said: "You'll stop in to say good-bye to us?"

"Of course."

Almost as soon as he was gone, Polly Wellman came in. He must have seen her approach and he had left the coast clear for her.

She looked fresh and neat and wholesome in a black polo shirt and a yellow dirndl skirt. She said hello with an open-mouthed smile.

"I hear you're leaving."

"Yes."

"Go right ahead and pack," she said. "Don't mind me."

I carried a box out to the car trunk. When I returned, Polly was sitting on the table. Her legs were crossed and one foot in a brown-and-white low-heeled shoe was swinging.

"Harry, will you be back?"

I was opening the valise on the floor. "Give me time."

Her foot stopped swinging. I didn't raise my eyes higher than her legs. They were bare and trim.

"Does that mean you'll be back?" she said.

It was too soon to know what I would do, what I wanted.

"I think so," I told her.

"I'll be waiting, Harry."